SEVEN DAYS

NICHOLE GREENE

❀ Created with Vellum

For all of us with quirofilia
IYKYK

PREFACE

This book contains discussions of loss of loved ones; parent, partner, and pregnancy.

1

BRIANNA

Seven seconds ago, I was happily engaged, blissfully unaware that my future husband wasn't just logging late hours at work; he was out fucking one of the partners' personal assistants. Standing beside our table at a busy cafe in West Hollywood, her big brown eyes fill with tears as she realizes he made her the other woman. Trevor sends her a derisive look, full of wrath, before turning his blue eyes back to mine. He opens his mouth to speak, but I throw my hand up. I had a feeling he was hiding something from me, and now my stomach churns with embarrassment as my pride and heart fall apart piece by piece.

Swinging my handbag over my shoulder, I stand to

leave, but the woman grabs my arm as mascara laced tears cut tracks down her cheeks.

"I had no idea."

"I believe you, and I don't blame you." I pull my arm from her grasp as I dig deep for the stoic mask I perfected years ago when I watched my mom die of cancer. It's been a long time since I needed my poker face, but I'm happy to know I can still pull it off.

"Brianna, wait," Trevor says as he stands to follow me.

I don't turn around as my pace increases, making my way past a large party on their way to be seated, knowing they'll be good cover for my escape. The hot afternoon June air envelops me as I dart out onto the sidewalk. I don't know where I'm going; I just need to find a place to hide out and think.

I walk a few blocks, happy with my choice to wear flats. Trevor probably would have been able to catch up with me eventually if I'd been in heels. I glance down an alley and see a sign for a place called The Generous Pour.

The weathered sign and poor location make it the perfect spot to hide away. He'll never think to look for me in a dive bar with an entrance off an alley. Pushing open the door, I walk into a nearly empty space. Movie posters from the 80s dot the walls and the sticky floor pulls at the soles of my flats as I cross to a long wooden bar lined with backless vinyl stools. Formica topped tables are spread out haphazardly throughout the rest of the room; two of them occupied by patrons who look like they could have slept in their seats.

I opt for a stool at the far end of the bar with a view of the front door, on the off chance Trevor comes looking in here. The bartender, a hipster with gauged ears and full sleeve tattoos on both arms, looks over at me skeptically. I give my head a slight shake so he knows not to come down yet.

I need to think. I can't go home. I moved in with Trevor after we got engaged last spring. Tears burn my eyes as I let myself think about the utter betrayal. He cheated on me. He was inside another woman. I'm so embarrassed and horrified.

God, this hurts.

My chest seizes as I imagine him with the slender blonde. She was pretty, the sort of common blonde that effortlessly exists in southern California. She's everything I'm not, with my dark hair and curvy body. It's the only thing I have left from my mom so I try to cherish it, even as I feel the looks from the shallow LA crowd.

Mentally, I run through the friends I could stay with. My best friend, Sara, has moved to DC for a Supreme Court clerkship so she's out. All my other friends are mutuals with Trevor and I can't for the life of me imagine trying to explain this situation to them. With a sigh, I pull my phone out and call the one person I can always count on, my dad.

"Hello, beautiful." His deep voice immediately comforts me and I can't hold the tears back.

I sniffle once and I feel him tense through the phone.

"What's wrong, sweet pea?" he asks as I try to fight back the sob that is desperately tearing at my throat.

"Trevor cheated on me." The words burn as they tumble from my lips. "I need somewhere to stay while I figure things out."

"That piece of shit," he growls. "I'm in Toronto for the next week and the house is being repainted."

"Fuck." The first tear falls along with all my hopes. "I can just check into a hotel. It'll be okay."

"Wait, let me check on a few things. Where are you now?"

"A dive bar in West Hollywood."

"Okay, stay there. Have a drink to calm down and read one of your alien books." He has never let me live down the fact that he found me reading a science fiction romance on vacation last winter. "I'm on this. Do you have a car?"

"No, Trevor drove." I motion for the bartender. "I can always just grab an Uber to a hotel, Dad. It's not a big deal."

"Give me ten minutes. I love you."

"I love you, too." I hit end on the call and look at the liquor lined up on the shelf behind the bartender. "Vodka Sprite with a splash of cranberry, please."

"No problem." He looks at me with just the smallest bit of compassion. He must have overheard my phone conversation.

I set my phone face up on the bar and look around The Generous Pour. Multi-colored Christmas lights are stapled around the top of the walls, and the yellow paint looks like it's seen better days. When my phone vibrates, drawing my attention, I grimace when I see Trevor's name and face appear on the screen. He's trying to FaceTime me, but I decline it.

The bartender sets my drink down in front of me along with a bowl of pretzels. "Want to talk about it?"

I put the glass to my lips and drink. I wince at the

strength of the cheap vodka and lick my lips. "I see how this place got its name."

The corner of his lips turn up in a smirk as he watches me take another drink. I give him an up and down glance, he looks like a West Coast Pete Davidson; drug addiction likely included. He's the complete opposite of Trevor, who wears suits and would rather die than let his skin be marked with ink.

"I don't want to talk about it," I say, finally answering his question. "I actually want to talk about anything else."

My phone vibrates loudly against the bar and I glance down to see Thomas Brennan's name flash across the screen.

My brows furrow as I accept the call, bringing the phone to my ear. "Hello?"

"Your dad just called to ask if I could come get you. I'm leaving my house in Palos Verdes now. Drop me a pin so I can find you." Even through the phone, his voice holds power as he barks orders at me.

"Okay." I take a trembling breath at the rush of relief I feel, knowing I'll be hidden where Trevor won't know where to look. "Thank you, Thomas."

"No problem, Bri," his voice softens just a bit. "Are you okay waiting for a couple of hours until I get to you?"

"Yeah, I'm just tucked away at a little dive bar."

"Okay. I'll be there as soon as I can."

The line goes dead before I can say goodbye and I immediately drop a pin before setting my phone face down, ringer off. Last I checked, I had four missed calls and seven texts from Trevor. I'm not interested in anything he has to say, though.

The vodka continues to burn its way down my throat as I numb myself to all the feelings I'm trying to compartmental-ize. If I let myself wallow, the pain could drown me. I feel less and less each time the bottom of my glass hits the scratched surface of the bar.

The minutes pass by as Danny, the bartender, gives me a second and then third drink. It turns out, he moved here from Ohio with his bandmates to try to get a record deal. They share a one bedroom apartment and work multiple jobs toward expenses on releasing their first album inde-pendently.

I'm just finishing off my fourth drink when the door opens and Thomas strides in. Even in casual golf clothes, he looks powerful. His wide shoulders fill the door frame as he scans the room, quickly finding me. A weird fluttering feeling fills my stomach as his green eyes meet mine.

He confidently crosses the room, his warm hand resting on my back as he stops beside me. "Ready to go?"

"Yeah," I say as I grab my phone and purse. "Just need to pay my tab."

"Don't worry about it," Danny says with a wave of his hand.

"You haven't had anyone other than me and those two tables all day," I say as I gesture around. "Let me pay so I can at least tip you."

"No." He shakes his head with a grin. "But you can come to the show I told you about in a couple weeks." He grabs a napkin and writes down his number. "Take this and give me a call sometime."

"Thanks." I drop the napkin in my purse and start digging for cash, but before I can even get my wallet out, Thomas has slapped a hundred dollar bill down.

"Let's get going." His hand splays across my back as I stumble clumsily off the stool. "How many of those did you have?"

"Not nearly enough," I mumble, noting the irritation coloring his question, as he guides me out the door and into his Porsche.

He slides a pair of silver aviators on and effortlessly maneuvers the car out of the alley, while I gather my hair into a quick and sloppy fishtail braid because he's got the top down. I must be drunker than I thought because Thomas seems much sexier than he ever has before. The light blue of his shirt contrasts with his perpetually tan skin, and his arms are corded with muscle, as are his thighs. I bet if I ran my hand over them they'd be firm and warm.

Why am I fantasizing about his thighs?

"Brianna?" His voice pulls me out of my dirty thoughts. "Did you hear me?"

"No, sorry." I slide my sunglasses on and look over at him. "What did you say?"

"I said don't vomit in my car. My housekeeper has the week off. I'm fine letting you stay with me, but I'm not interested in playing nursemaid to your feelings."

How this blunt asshole is my dad's best friend, I'll never understand. They are the definition of opposites attract. My dad is a warm, loving, cinnamon roll of a man. Thomas Brennan is as cold as he is beautiful.

"Noted." I can't stop the sarcastic tone in my voice from seeping out. Luckily he pulls out onto the highway effectively cutting our conversation.

2

BRIANNA

"Help yourself to anything in the house," Thomas says as he pulls into the driveway. "The guest room is the first on the right, down the second hallway. I have a tee time in twenty minutes. I'll be back later."

I've barely closed the car door before he pulls back out of the driveway, leaving me to make my way through the garage, past his Lamborghini, Range Rover, and Harley. I haven't been inside this house. He moved here a few years ago from Laguna Beach and the house I'd visited more times than I could count with my dad.

I manage to find my way to the kitchen, which is open to a light, airy living room. It barely looks lived in, but the delicious, spicy scent of his cologne lingers in the space. There are no dishes in the sink; not even a coffee cup. No bananas on the counter . . . Just a sterile, spotless space. I guess it shouldn't surprise me; he is a surgeon after all. He's probably a neat freak.

A bachelor neat freak.

I step around the island and find a small wine refrigerator. Crouching down, I pull open the door and grab the first bottle I come to. It's a bottle of champagne. Drinking this on an empty stomach after all the vodka is probably a bad idea, but I think I'm owed a get out of jail free card today.

I pull the foil off the top and pop the cork, startling as it flies across the room and ricochets off one of the massive sliding doors leading out to the pool. I can't believe I didn't notice the view. Wandering over to the door, I slide one open.

The warm early summer air envelops me as I step out onto the concrete of the pool deck. The pool is long and narrow, running the length of the back property line and I can see the entire arc of the Queen's Necklace and all the beaches from Laguna to Malibu, from his backyard. High hedge-like trees block the yard from the neighbors view. I can see why he bought this property.

Swigging champagne from the bottle, I sit down on the edge of the pool, letting my feet dangle in the water, which is the perfect temperature.

If I had a swimsuit, I'd probably jump in. I can't remember the last time I went for a swim. Maybe two summers ago on vacation with Trevor's family in Miami. He made a really hurtful joke about my body fitting in more with women on South Beach than in Los Angeles, a dig at the curves my Brazilian mother gave me. You would think the man would appreciate this body, but he'd find ways to give me subtle digs all the time.

I should strip down and go for a swim.

Fuck Trevor.

I press my lips to the bottle and take another drink, loving the way the bubbles dance on my tongue. The sun is still high in the sky and I know golf can take hours, so I probably have time to take a short dip. I giggle to myself at how appalled Trevor would be to know I'm about to skinny-dip in my dad's best friend's pool.

That thought fuels my decision as I stand and pull my sundress over my head. Grabbing my phone and setting it by the bottle, I push my panties down my legs and unhook my bra. Jumping into the cool water with a splash, I stay beneath the surface, swimming to the infinity edge before coming up for air and peering down at the crashing waves below.

I stay there for a while, mesmerized by the waves hitting the rocks. Falling into thoughts of Trevor's betrayal, I search my mind for any obvious signs that I missed. There has to have been something, some clue to give away his shady behavior.

The longer I wrack my brain, the less I can think of. We're both so busy, with me finishing my second year of law school and him starting his new job as a junior associate. Maybe we just fell out of love. Am I even really sad? When I think about him cheating I'm mostly humiliated. There's not really any pain now that the shock has worn off. Was I even in love with him at all?

My phone starts to ring so I push off the wall and swim to the other side. It's a FaceTime call from Sara. I click accept, after making sure she can't see my tits.

"I really need to know why Trevor just texted me asking if I had talked to you. And why are you naked in a pool I've never seen before?" Her eyebrows nearly touch her hairline as she holds my gaze in the no nonsense way that will make her an incredible attorney.

"He texted you because I'm ignoring him."

"Why?" she demands.

"We were at brunch and his side piece came up to us demanding answers."

"No!" Her eyes widen as the news sinks in.

"Yes." I nod my head and put the bottle back to my lips. "I remember seeing her around at parties. She is one of the partners' PAs."

"What a fucking moron. Has he seen you? Has he spoken to you? Fucking gorgeous and brilliant. Honestly, it's his loss."

"Yeah, I don't know. I don't want to think about him. I'm giving myself the night to make bad decisions."

"Speaking of bad decisions, where are you?" She squints at the screen, probably trying to figure out based on the view.

"Dad's out of town and having the house repainted so I can't stay there. I was just going to grab a hotel room but he called Thomas to come to get me. I guess I'm staying here for the week while I wait for dad to get home."

"You, my bestie, are skinny dipping in your dad's best friend's pool? In the middle of the day for anyone to see? Who are you?"

"No one can see me," I flip the camera around for her so she sees what I see. "And he's out golfing, I'm here alone."

"That's a sexy view."

"Right? I can't believe he lives here all alone."

"He's a plastic surgeon, right? I doubt he spends much time alone."

A weird feeling hits my chest as she makes the insinuation about him bringing women home. It must be the champagne getting to me.

"Probably. I hope he doesn't bring anyone around while I'm here. I don't need reminders that other people are in happy relationships, fuck buddy-ships, or even casual one night stands."

"Bright side, you don't have to fake orgasms anymore."

I cackle. "So true. I just break out my vibe, orgasm, and go on about my day now. It's not a whole production."

"This is why we're besties. Always reminding each other about the silver linings." She looks off to the side and nods her head at someone. "Bri, I have to go, but maybe you should come out here for a few weeks. Get out of California, some distance. You'll love DC."

"Thanks, I'll think about it. I want to regroup with Dad first. Maybe after that."

"Okay, sounds good. I love you."

"Love you, too."

I set my phone down and decide to swim a few lazy laps. It feels good to move, even though I'm sluggish from all the alcohol. As I start to get winded , I flip onto my back, just floating as the sun beats down on my naked body. I stay like that until I start to feel myself drifting off.

I should probably get out anyway, I don't need Thomas coming home to find me naked in his pool. The thought of it does make me wonder what he would do. Would he be upset? Would he be turned on? That's a ridiculous thought. He has spent his life surgically sculpting women into perfect bodies. He'd probably look at me, be appalled, and start imagining all the ways he could improve my figure.

It's not that I think there's anything wrong with me. This body is my mom's legacy and I embrace it. I love the way my body curves and my soft belly, just like all the women from that side of my family. But living in LA seriously fucks with your concept of a normal, healthy body. Trevor didn't help in that regard, either.

Swimming over to the side, I lift myself out. I really should have looked for a towel before jumping in the pool. I don't want to track water into the house, so I lay out on one of the lounge chairs to air dry. My eyes drift shut as the warmth of the sun seeps into me, lulling me into a deep sleep, filled with flashes of strong hands and thrusting bodies.

I jerk awake at the sound of a car horn in the distance. The skin on my back feels tight as I roll onto my side and I can feel the dry stinging of a mild burn with the movement. My eyes widen as I realize it's nearly dark outside, but I relax a bit when I see the lights are still off in the house, and the door from the living to the pool deck is still open like I left it.

Chills race over my skin from the cooling night air as I race to pick up my belongings and the discarded champagne bottle before darting into the house. I set the bottle on the counter and head down the hall to the guest room Thomas said I could stay in.

The room is as sterile as the rest of the house. Whoever decorated this place needs to figure out how to incorporate color. Everything is white, except for sparse pops of navy in the bedding and a painting on the wall.

The en suite bathroom is beautiful, but as bland as everything else. Marble lines the floor and walls, and the gold veins in the stone are highlighted by the contemporary gold fixtures. The towels are plush and navy, pulling the theme from the bedroom into the bathroom.

Finding a mirror, I turn and look at my back, wincing at the burn turning my backside reddish-pink from its usual bronze. I decide a cool shower would be beneficial, so I step under the rain shower head and leave the water as cold as I can handle. Usually, I prefer lava hot temperatures so this is extra uncomfortable.My mind wanders to my dream as I wash my hair and body quickly using the travel-size toiletry bottles already in the shower. I haven't had a dream in ages, let alone a sex dream. It's odd that I would have one now, on the night that I found out my fiancé was cheating on me. Must have been the champagne.

By the time I step out of the shower and dry off, I still haven't heard Thomas return and the sky out the window is nearly dark, with only the tiniest bit of pink lingering over the Pacific. I check the closet and drawers to see if there are any clothes I can borrow but everything is depressingly empty.

With nothing else to do, I pull down the cool covers and climb onto the bed. My mind keeps falling into the trap of thinking about Trevor and it's driving me crazy. I'm so aggravated seeing his face and replaying memories. What would really piss him off to see me doing right now?

I could masturbate. Nothing offended him more than when I would get myself off. The more I sit with the idea, the more I love it. He never made me come, and while I faked it for him, he did realize that I could get myself off much faster and easier than he could.

Letting my mind go back to the bits I remember of the dream earlier, I recall the beautiful hands with weathered skin and long, elegant fingers. I bet they'd feel incredible tracing my curves. I ghost my fingertips through the valley of my breasts and then along the bottom swell and back to my nipples, squirming as I tease them, focusing on the pleasure of the light touches.

I keep teasing my breasts as heat builds in my core. Pressing my thighs together, I arch my back off the bed as I run my hands down my belly to my center. I'm already wet, picturing those mystery hands teasing my slit and I run my fingers along the bare skin of my pussy before rubbing a light circle over my clit.

My breaths come faster as I imagine being filled by the faceless man from my dreams, and I let my legs fall open, increasing my pressure and speed. I bite down on my lip as I whimper, the edge of my orgasm inching closer and closer.

I imagine my legs wrapped around his waist as he thrusts into me with hard, fast strokes, saying my name in a voice that seems familiar, gruff and stern. While his hips continue to pump into me, I look into his green eyes and call out Thomas' name as I come, my pussy fluttering around my drenched fingers.

3

THOMAS

While I was out on the golf course I got an alert on my phone that the back door had been opened. I disabled the alarm and slid my phone into my pocket, not giving it a thought. But as I was loading my clubs in the trunk, I decided to check and see if she had gone back in because I still had an alert about the open door.

There she was, floating naked in my pool. I was mildly alarmed when it looked like she was falling asleep, especially when I noticed the empty champagne bottle beside her. I was planning on stopping for some groceries and picking up takeout for dinner, but decided I'd better get home before she accidentally drowned in my pool.

By the time I got home, she had come in. As I passed her

room, I heard the shower running. I realized she didn't have clothes with her so went to grab some from my room.

Now, I'm standing at the threshold of the guest room watching Brianna, writhing around in the sheets, her fingers pumping into her pussy as she comes with my name on her lips.

What the hell?

Fuck, but she's gorgeous. Her body is a literal work of art. Though I couldn't see her well on the camera, I can now. And I didn't even think twice about seeing a naked woman, I look at them nearly every day. But seeing her tan skin and brown nipples illuminated in the light of the moon does something to me. Her black hair spills across the white pillows like an onyx river, making me want to run my fingers through it.

But her pussy. *Fuck*. It's perfect.

My cock is rock hard, pressing against the zipper of my shorts. This is so wrong. She's my best friend's daughter. Who just found out her dickhead ex was cheating on her. I just wanted to bring her some sweats and a t-shirt until we can get to her apartment and pick up her things tomorrow.I didn't know I'd be getting treated to a peep show instead and I haven't been this hard in years. Her entire body undulates as she comes. It is impossible to tear my eyes away.

Brianna must realize she came thinking about me because she mumbles to herself, too low for me to hear. She rolls onto her side away from me as she lifts the covers up and over her. I should set the clothes on the floor by the door and walk away, but I can't. Something drives me to keep watch over her until I hear the soft sounds of sleep coming.

Pushing the door open softly, I set the clothes on the dresser. A moment passes while I fight the desire to walk around the far side of the bed and look down on her. I lie to myself, convincing no one that I'm just going around to check on her.

I am worried.

I'm just more drawn to her than I should be. As I cross the room and step beside the bed I see her full lips gently parted. Despite the orgasm she just had, her brows are furrowed and her face looks sad. Sadder than I've seen her since I walked into that dive bar. I haven't even seen her shed one tear yet, and it takes every bit of will power I possess to not smooth her brow out with my thumb.

Who am I right now? This isn't me. I don't do tender feelings. I sure as fuck shouldn't be lusting over my best friend's daughter. Yet here I am, tempted to glide my hands over her sinful curves and smooth skin.

She shifts onto her back and I freeze, hoping she won't wake up to find me looming over her like some sort of pervert. I manage to creep back to the door without her waking, closing softly behind me.

My feet move quietly over the cool marble tiles down the hall to my bedroom. I head directly for the bathroom, ready to shower off the sweat from the eighteen holes I played. Pulling my shirt over my head, I look at my reflection in the mirror a little harder than usual.

I've taken good care of myself over the years. Anything I would tell my patients to do to prevent needing my services,

I've done. I'm fanatic about using sunscreen, drinking enough water, and getting adequate exercise. That dedication shows in my physique, there aren't many fifty year old men with firm pectorals and defined abs.

As I step into the shower, I consider taking a cold one. My dick is still painfully hard, but it feels wrong to jerk off to thoughts of my best friend's daughter.

My.

Best.

Friend's.

Daughter.

Who I have known since she was nine. Never, not once, have I ever looked at her with a lustful thought. Obviously, she's beautiful, but so what? Beautiful women are a dime a dozen in southern California.

The harder I try not to think about her, the more I fixate, and before I realize what I'm doing, my hand is wrapped around my cock as I relive the sounds Bri made as she circled her clit. How her pussy was so wet I could hear it from outside the room as she pumped her fingers in and out of her greedy, little cunt. The way she arched her back as she came, crying out my name.

My hand works faster, moving up and down my shaft with ruthless strokes. The rougher the better as far I'm concerned. I deserve a broken dick for this.

I picture her full tits and perfect nipples, imagining attaching a pair of clamps to them. Tugging on them as her orgasm builds. Thrusting my cock into her instead of my palm. I brace my left hand on the shower wall as I cum with an intensity I've not experienced in so long it feels foreign.

My chest heaves as I rest my head against the wall. Self-loathing runs deep through me, churning my stomach with bitter bile. Guilt eats at me, knowing Jack called me to take care of his daughter while he was away and here I am, twelve hours later, thinking about her while I jerk off in the shower.

I wash up quickly, ready to leave the shower of shame as fast as fucking possible. I dry off and pull on some athletic shorts before getting into bed. I brought home some charts to look over, but I don't think I can concentrate on anything right now. I just need to sleep so I can wake up in the morning and forget what I saw.

"Good morning," Bri says as she walks into the kitchen.

"Morning." I grab another mug and pour a cup of coffee for her. It's wrong to notice how adorable she is in my t-shirt and sweat pants but, fuck it, she is. Her long, dark hair is piled on top of her head. Her flawless bronze skin is completely free of makeup. It's refreshing to see so much natural beauty.

"Thanks for the clothes. I didn't even hear you come home last night." The slightest blush highlights her cheeks. Her luminous brown eyes look past me as I slide her a cup of coffee. "Thank you, for the coffee, too."

"I have today off if you want to drive to your apartment and get your things. Pick up your car?" I pull eggs out of the refrigerator.

"Oh, that's great. Trevor is supposed to be up in San

Francisco today and tomorrow for meetings." She catches her bottom lip between her teeth as she watches me beat a few eggs for us. "Are you sure it's not a problem? I can always grab an Uber up to my apartment. I don't want you to waste your day off on me."

What she doesn't know is that I canceled an entire day of consultations for her. I texted my office manager on the way to the golf course to let her know. Now that I've had graphic fantasies about her, I'm wondering if spending an entire day alone with her is the smartest move, but I can be on my best behavior.

Last night never happened.

I didn't come thinking about her wrapped around me.

She probably doesn't even remember fantasizing about me.

"Don't worry about it. I told Jack I'd help you out this week so I will." I try to keep my tone polite but aloof. I shouldn't even entertain these thoughts of me and her.

"Can I help with anything?" She glances at the avocados and bread I have out on the island.

"Sure." I roll an avocado to her. "Slice this up. I figured we could have avocado toast with our eggs."

"Sounds good." She leans forward to reach for the cutting board and knife and as she does her shirt hangs just low enough for me to catch a glimpse of tantalizing tan skin.

Jesus Christ.

Eyes on breakfast.

Luckily, she gets a text and taps out a response. It obviously isn't her idiot ex because she's smirking at the phone.

The text exchange lasts a couple minutes as she gets her task finished.

We eat quickly and silently. I could be warmer to her, but if I open that door it might lead to deeper conversation. Deeper conversation could lead to intellectual attraction and that coupled with the physical pull I already feel for her would be bad news all around.

I text Jack to let him know what we're doing while she gets her purse.

ME: I'm taking Bri to get her things from her apartment

Jack: Good. Punch the slimy bastard in the face if you see him.

Me: Consider it done.

Jack: How is she?

Me: She's holding up. I anticipate the packing will be emotional.

Jack: Maybe. She learned how to shut her feelings off when Lucia passed away.

Jack: It's easy for her to disassociate and compart-mentalize.

Me: I'll keep a closer eye on her, then.

Jack: Appreciate it

4

BRIANNA

The drive is painfully quiet, NPR playing softly as he maneuvers the Range Rover through traffic. I try to pay attention to a story about climate change, but my mind keeps wandering to last night.I can't believe how hard I came thinking about him. Walking into the kitchen this morning and seeing him dressed so casually in black athletic shorts and a tight white t-shirt had my stomach doing a weird flip.

How does he look so damn good at his age? I know he's a few years younger than my dad, but still, I swear I could see ab definition. And don't even get me started on his arms and hands. I guess a surgeon would need to have steady hands, but his are aged in a way that makes me think he knows what he is doing beyond the operating room.

He certainly knew what he was doing in my fantasy.

I squirm in my seat, squeezing my legs together. It's so incredibly inappropriate to be lusting over my dad's best friend, a man over twice my age, as he drives me to my apartment.

Maybe that's why I'm so fixated on Thomas. To avoid thinking about the emotional task in front of me. I know it won't be easy to walk into our apartment and pack up my belongings. Our apartment always smells like Trevor's cologne. He picked most of the furniture, buying it with his first few paychecks. At least I won't have to worry about moving anything big.

My ring catches the light, the reflection bouncing around the interior of the car, and melancholy fills my soul as I look down at my hand. I did love him. I loved this ring. I loved our life and the potential of what we had together. Heat burns my eyes as my chest constricts and a small sob breaks through as I fight back the tears. Thomas reaches down into the center console and hands me a tissue. Thankfully, he does all of it without taking his eyes off the road. I hate letting people see me cry.

Crumpling up the tissue in my hand, I look out the window as we get closer to LA, blinking to clear the remaining tears. I jump, startled when Thomas's hand reaches over and squeezes my thigh.

"It'll be okay," his deep voice rumbles between us. "He's an idiot for cheating on you."

I manage to nod and give him a tremulous smile. Despite being upset, heat pools in my belly as his hand lingers, the heat seeping through the material of the sweatpants I borrowed from him. A part of me wishes I could feel his skin against mine.

Rolling my lip between my teeth, I allow myself to think back to last night after my shower. I don't understand why it was his body I imagined against me, inside me. Clearly, I just haven't been fucked well enough lately. Add to that the fact that I'm staying in his house and everything screams his name. I mean, fuck, every room of the place smells like his expensive cologne. Even the clean clothes I'm wearing.

I fight the urge to pout when he pulls his hand away from my leg. It's almost like he forgot for a minute that he was touching me. With his left hand relaxed on the wheel and his right resting on the gearshift, he exudes a sort of effortlessly confident masculinity. Aside from his watch, there's nothing that screams wealth about him.

He's exceptionally handsome, though. His once jet black hair has a few strands of silver threaded through, but it doesn't age him. His deep green eyes, straight roman nose, and perfect lips make a striking profile along with his sharp jaw. His eyes crinkle in the corner when he gives a rare smile.

We pull up to my building and I hand him the card that opens the door to the underground parking garage, directing him to the loading bay parking area. He puts his hand on my lower back as we step onto the elevator but, as I hit the button for my floor, nerves take off inside me.

"What if Trevor didn't go on his work trip?" I blurt out the question as my stomach turns.

"You don't have to worry about him with me here, okay?" Thomas turns me and tilts my head back with his finger under my chin. "I'll keep him away from you while you pack."

He waits until I answer with a nod before dropping his hand and eye contact. He motions for me to go first when the elevator opens and I lead us down the hall until we come to my door. My hand shakes as I push the key inside the lock, but Thomas leans against the wall and gives me as much time as I need.

I don't know what will be on the other side of this door. An angry fiancé? A regretful one? It doesn't matter, because the one thing I will never tolerate is infidelity. He could drop to his knees and kiss my toes and it wouldn't change a damn thing.

I push the door open with a deep breath. Blessed silence greets me as I cross the threshold into the wide hallway that leads past the bedroom and office and into the living area. Pulling open the hall closet, I see his suitcase is missing. Good. He did go. I grab every remaining piece of luggage and drag them into the bedroom, setting them on the bed and opening them up.

"Do you want help?" Thomas asks from where he fills the door frame.

I look around the room and try to think of what he could help with. "You want to go through and grab the photos that belong to me? Just the ones with Mom and Dad."

"I can do that," he says before disappearing down the hall.

I busy myself in the closet, grabbing my clothes in armfuls and dumping them into suitcases. Even though I know Trevor is out of town I want to limit my time here. If I pause too long, I'll feel all the emotions I'm trying to fight back. I don't want to cry. I don't want to feel this hurt. I just want to stay numb until it's so far past it feels more like a blip than a broken heart.

My phone dings in my purse and I fish it out, dropping it when I see Trevor's face on the screen. He's FaceTiming me. For a second I think about just declining it, but then I realize he should see me packing up my things from our apartment.

"Hello?" My tone is as cold as ice.

"Brianna, thank fuck you finally answered." His blond hair is perfectly sculpted the way he likes, but his mouth is set in a straight line. "I know it looks bad, but it's not what you think and you can't just run off like that. Where'd you even go?"

"Somewhere safe." I make a show of packing for him to see. "How did you know I was back here?"

"I turned on my desk webcam to watch for you. What are you doing?" he asks incredulously.

"Getting my things out of the apartment. I'll be completely gone by the end of the day." I can't believe he turned on a camera in here to watch and wait for me.

"You can't be serious." He's practically yelling at me now. "It's not that big of a deal. You don't have anywhere to go."

"I have plenty of places to go. Thousands, really." I look him dead in the eye, making sure to stay as emotionless as possible. "Anywhere where you're not, is a perfectly fine place for me. Goodbye, Trevor."

My eyes heat with oncoming tears as I hit end on the call. Giving myself three minutes to cry and feel sorry for myself, I let them roll down my cheeks, swiping them away as quickly as they come. When I look at the clock and see my time is up, I force myself off the bed and back to the closet.

My reflection in the closet mirror catches my eye and I realize I'm still wearing Thomas's clothes. Without giving it too much thought, I pull one of my favorite sundresses off a hanger and slip it on. It's just a yellow linen halter dress, simple, but the color really works with my skin tone. I rarely wore it because Trevor didn't like it.

Thomas is zipping up some of my full suitcases, a stack of picture frames beside him, when I finally finish getting the last of my toiletries packed up. He picks up a photo from Trevor's bedside table and looks at it.

"Does he really have a framed photo of just himself beside the bed?" He looks over at me with a raised eyebrow.

"Yeah." I cringe, knowing how it looks seeing the photo I took of him at his law school graduation. I asked him about why he didn't put one of the two of us together in the frame instead. He said he worked hard to make it into and through law school. That he deserved to see a reminder of it every day.

"Wow." He sets it down with a disgusted look on his face. "He seems like a great guy."

Right as he finishes that statement my phone vibrates with a text from Trevor.

TREVOR: Who is the guy?

Trevor: What are you doing, Brianna?

Trevor: ANSWER ME

I SEND him a middle finger emoji before blocking his number. Muttering to myself, I walk out of the bedroom and into the open area where Trevor's desk is. I should have turned the camera off as soon as I hung up with him.

I'm bent over the desk, trying to figure out how to turn off the webcam when I feel Thomas at my back. His hand lands on my waist and squeezes gently. My entire body is vibrating with a toxic combination of anger, frustration, and hurt as I fumble with the keys.

"Bri," his hand covers mine, "talk to me. Tell me what's going on."

His breath is warm on my bare shoulder as he speaks andI stand up, but don't turn around. His presence at my back feels comforting, like I could lean against it and let him hold me up. "Trevor has this webcam on. He's been watching it and waiting for me to come home."

I bang a few keys in frustration trying to figure out how to log onto his computer.

"This camera?" he asks quietly as he points at the lens.

"Yeah." I nod.

Thomas doesn't move and I swear I can feel him thinking behind me. I just wish I knew what was going through his head.

"He's watching now?"

The hand that was on my waist moves up my ribcage. My nipples tighten as I feel his lips graze my neck and my body rocks back against his as I draw in a shaky breath.

"I have an idea, but I need you to consent to me touching you." His hand moves to right below my breast and his thumb slowly caresses the swell. "What do you say, Bri? Shall we show him what a real orgasm looks like on a woman?"

I take another deep breath before answering. "Yes." I nod. "Please."

Oh my God. Is this really happening?

5

THOMAS

It's over as soon as I hear 'please' leave her lips in that breathy whisper. I call on all my will power to not strip her all the way down and fuck her ruthlessly against her ex's desk. Instead, I move painfully slowly, my fingertips finding her nipples through her dress. I draw light, teasing circles around them until I know they're hard enough to show through the material. I want this asshole to see exactly how good I make her feel.

One hand slips under the strap of her dress and my dick surges to life against the curve of her ass. She isn't wearing a bra, there's nothing to put a barrier between us. Her chest rises and falls with deep breaths as I slide the strap all the way to the side, exposing her along with what I'm doing to her to the camera.

I'm punching my ticket straight to hell for this and fuck if I care. Looking down at her body and feeling the weight of her breast in my palm erases every sane thought from my head. She releases the slightest whimper as I continue the soft, teasing strokes around her nipple.

My other hand moves slowly down her soft belly, over her rounded hip, and down her thigh. Her legs are pressed tightly together. I begin bunching her skirt up with my fingers, inching it slowly up her legs.

"Spread your legs for me, Siren." I kiss her neck as I whisper the instructions.

She does what I ask immediately and it makes me that much harder. Alarm bells are screaming in my mind, but my need for her overcomes all of that. I keep my pace slow, despite my desire to drive my fingers into her until she's screaming my name again. Trailing my hand lightly up her thigh, I cup her pussy.

The soft lace is noticeably damp as I move my fingers back and forth lazily. I tease her where the edges of her panties lie. She's bare and so fucking soft, everywhere I touch. I moan against her neck as I slip a finger under the edge and drag it along her drenched folds.

She shivers as I begin to tease her clit. Her head falls back on my shoulder, her lips parted as she rocks against my hand.

"Thomas," she says my name on a groan, "fuck, that feels so good."

"Good. Let me take care of you."

I want so badly to kiss her. To take her lips and inhale

her pleasure. To own every part of her body as she falls apart in my hands.

She catches her lip between her teeth and looks up at me, her pupils expand as I slide two fingers inside her. Her eyes move to my lips and back up. She wants to kiss me just as much as I do her, but she turns her head.

I explore her body with eager hands, learning what her tells are when I do something right. From this angle I can easily stimulate her g-spot. Her startled gasp as I start tapping it makes me think no one else has ever found it before. I'll give her as many new sensations as she'll allow.

I increase the speed and intensity of everything I'm doing. Her hands grip both forearms, holding on tight as she climbs higher and higher. I can feel her arousal dripping down my fingers and the need to taste her rages through me like a wildfire.

When her walls clamp down on my fingers, I work her pretty little pussy straight through the best orgasm she's ever had. She cries out as her legs go weak, slumping against me as I stroke her clit while she rides the aftershocks.

I withdraw my hands and right her clothing as she catches her breath. Her cheeks are pink as she turns and looks up at me. She looks just as surprised as I am at what just happened. I wish I could tell if she regretted it. Her eyes dip to my lips for a split second again and I take a step back. I want to kiss her. But if I kissed her now I would take her now. I need to figure things out. I need to think logically about this. As does she.

I watch as she turns around and unplugs the monitor, effectively turning off the camera. She looks back at me, her face burning. "I guess I could have done that and saved us from having to do, uh," she gestures at her body as she stumbles over her words, "all that."

Part of me wants to push her. Wants to ask what she means by 'all that', but the part of me that wants her again is pulling the reins.

WE PACKED up both her car and mine with bags and a few boxes of personal items without making eye contact. I felt her eyes on me a few times and I sure as shit was looking at her every time her back was turned.

The whole drive back to my house I've been wondering what's going through her head. Is she okay? Does she regret that? I can unequivocally say that I do not regret one second. Holding that goddess-like body of hers in my arms while I made her come all over my hand. I can smell her sweet, musky scent on me still.

I want more. I want to drive my cock deep inside her. I want to taste her honey cunt. I want to listen to her come apart over and over for me.

Guilt-ridden thoughts of Jack filter into my mind. When he picked up the phone and asked me to go pick Bri up I'm sure he didn't mean this. This would end our friendship of over fifteen years.

Thoughts of Bri volley back and forth in my mind. Desire and hunger for her on one hand. Shame and guilt for even considering doing more than what we've already done on the other. I hit the button to open the gate and garage.

Taking a steadying breath as I get out of the car, I wonder what the best way to approach this is. Be direct or let her lead? Apparently I won't have to decide because she's striding across the driveway toward me. I hit close on the gate keypad as I watch her approach.

"Thomas." She stops about four feet away, backlit by the sun.

"Bri."

"You're my dad's best friend."

"I am."

"I just ended my engagement yesterday."

"I remember."

"This is wrong." Despite her words she steps closer. "Like really fucking forbidden wrong."

"Yes." This time I step closer to her. Her pulse is hammering in her neck, a siren's call for my lips. I can read the desire all over her face, but I'm going to make her ask for it. "But?"

"But," she swallows as she holds my gaze, "I want more."

"More what?"

"You. Orgasms. What you did back in my apartment was," she trails off as she searches for the words, "the most erotic experience of my life."

A slow smile splits my face. "That was just me getting started. What I want to do to you will blow your mind and ruin you for anyone else." I cup her face in the palm of my hand and rub my thumb over her lips. "If we do this, you're mine for the week. Seven days only."

"No strings, just fucking," she whispers before her tongue darts out to lick her lip.

I nod as my fingers slip into her hair.

"Ruin me." Her eyes find mine as her words unleash the feral beast within me.

I pull her hair at the roots, tilting her head back so my mouth can crash down on hers. Her lips part as I slide my tongue past them. She tastes like peppermint and vanilla chapstick. Spinning us, I press her against the nearest hard surface, my Range Rover. Her hips buck against my hard length between us.

Untying the straps around her neck, I move my body away from her as the yellow material falls to the floor of my garage. She stands there, naked aside from a pair of light pink panties and her sandals, in the middle of my garage. Her eyes never leave mine, even as mine devour the sight before me with a fervent hunger.

She wraps her legs around my waist as I lift her into my arms and carry her into the house. The desire to fuck her right against the first wall I find is hard to deny, but the things I want to do to her require a bed. She asked to be ruined and ruination is exactly what she's going to get. Her ass and legs are so soft under my hands. I lose all rational thought when she shifts against me, her pussy grinding against my cock as she moans from pleasure at the friction. She kisses my neck with hot, sexy licks and nips.

I've never been so turned on in my life.

She squeals when I toss her onto the middle of my bed. At some point she kicked off her shoes but she still has that little scrap of lace covering her. Deciding to slow the pace down I run my hands up her legs, enjoying the way my light touch causes goosebumps to race across her flesh.

As I spread her legs apart I notice how wet her panties are already.

Gripping her by the hips, I drag her body back down to the edge of the bed where I can have full access.

"Have your panties been this wet for me since we put on a show back at your apartment?" I ask as I run my finger under the edge.

"They've been this wet for you since you picked me up from the bar yesterday." Her eyes have darkened to almost black with want as she answers me with refreshing honesty.

"Fuck," I growl as I bend to bury my face in her sweet cunt.

I planned to tease her, but fuck that. I tear her panties off and fling them over my shoulder before diving into her. My eyes nearly roll back in my head as I get the first taste of her. I circle her clit with my tongue as I slide two fingers back into her wet heat. Her hips buck as I nip and suck every part of her goddamn perfect pussy.

Time to begin the process of ruining her for anyone else. I keep my mouth on her clit, driving her right to the edge of orgasm and then backing off, over and over until she's begging to come. When we've both had enough of that torture, I slide my fingers into her and curl them toward her g-spot. She's a writhing, panting, moaning mess beneath me and she has no idea what's coming next.

6

BRIANNA

My back arches off the bed as Thomas works my clit and g-spot in tandem. Sweat rolls down my temples from the way he's been teasing me. Grinding against him as I slide my fingers through his dark hair, I think I'm on the precipice of the most intense orgasm of my life. When he adds pressure with the palm of his hand directly over my pelvis, I explode.

"Oh, God," I cry out over and over as wave after wave of blinding, hot pleasure rips through me. He never relents; licking and stroking me through the slowly diminishing pleasure.

"I am god-like, but you can just scream my name next time." He stands to his full height, still fully clothed and moves my boneless body up the bed, resting my head on a pillow.

When he pulls his shirt over his head and drops it on the floor beside him, I'm completely taken aback by the insanely good body he hides under his clothes. With wide shoulders and a chest with sculpted muscles, the most incredible thing is how defined his abs are. I've rarely seen twenty five year old guys with bodies like this.

He pushes his shorts down, taking his underwear with them. His cock is perfect, long and thick with a slight curve up. He crawls on top of me, taking my lips in a soft, sensual kiss. I can taste myself on him and it's intoxicating. His lips and tongue are so much gentler than our earlier passion fueled kisses.

"Are you okay?" he asks as he kisses down my neck.

"Yes." I run my fingers through his silky strands. "Are you?"

"I'm better than I have been in a very long time, Bri." His green eyes lock on mine. "Reach into the nightstand and pull out a condom."

He runs his fingers over my body as I reach over and fish one out. I gasp as he slides three thick fingers inside me. He watches them as he pumps in and out of me slowly.

"Put the condom on me," he commands.

My hands tremble as I open the foil wrapper. I wrap my hand around him and give him a few firm strokes. I look up at him as I swipe my thumb over his tip, gathering the bead of pre-cum and bringing it to my mouth. His eyes darken as he watches me suck it off.

"I'm going to fuck that mouth soon enough, but right

now, I need this cunt wrapped around my cock. Put the condom on and quit playing games." He grabs my wrists as soon as I finish and plants them beside my head as he pushes inside me in one hard thrust. I've never felt so full before. My jaw goes slack as he moans, pausing to take in the feeling of our joined bodies.

Thomas kisses me as he increases the speed of his thrusts, but keeps them shallow. The more I squirm beneath him to take him deeper the more he holds back. His teasing denial only serves to drive my want for him into a frenzied need and his fingers link with mine as I whimper beneath him. My nipples drag across his chest as I arch up into him.

"Please," I beg. "Harder, deeper."

"Fuck," he says with a growl.

He sits back, kneeling between my legs and lifts my hips into the air, giving himself all the leverage he needs to go deep. His fingers dig into my skin as he lets go and fucks me with an animalistic intensity.

Every slide of his cock hits the spot inside me that sends stars across my vision. His skin slaps against mine, and my pussy is so wet I can feel my desire streaming out of me. I clamp down on his dick as he circles my clit with his thumb, heating my body from my core out in pulsing waves of debilitating pleasure. I can barely breathe as I cry out his name.

He pushes all the way in, holding me by the waist as his cock surges inside me, and I can feel every twitch he makes as he empties himself. When I look down, I find him staring at where he's seated inside me. His eyes are unreadable when he finally looks into mine.

Pulling out of me slowly, Thomas gets off the bed with a slight frown before disappearing into the bathroom. Is he upset with me? I hear the sink running in the bathroom and a few minutes later he walks out with a warm cloth in his hand and a troubled look on his face.

"Are you mad?" I ask quietly.

He looks up at me with a confused expression on his face. "No, why would I be mad?"

"You're not talking and you frowned as you left me." My heart squeezes as I say the final three words.

"What is there to say? Do you need praise? I left to help you get cleaned up." He says the harsh words as he runs the warm cloth over me, gently cleaning me. "We need to go soon."

"Go where?" I ask as I grab the cloth from his hands. I can do it myself if he's going to turn into an asshole about it.

"We have an hour to make it to my office and get your blood and urine samples sent to the lab for an STI check." His delivery is cold and clinical. "I'm not fucking you again until I can do so without a condom. Are you on birth control?"

"Who says I even want you to fuck me again?" His words make sense, it's completely logical to get tested considering what I just found out, but he doesn't have to be such an asshole about it. "With that attitude I'll just go to the county health department and have them run the tests."

I stand and stride past him, as aloof as I can be, considering I'm still naked, but he grabs my arm.

"Stop." He guides me back to the bed. "I could have phrased that better. I apologize." He scrubs a hand over his face. "I just need a minute to think. Honestly, you need to be tested and I can fast track the results for you. We'll know by tomorrow."

I hesitate before answering. "You might be twice my age, but I'm a third year law student with a brain just as big and logical as yours. Never speak to me like that again. I'm done being talked down to." I walk past him and start down the hall. "I'm going to take a shower."

"Okay, I'll bring your bags in and set them in your room."

"Thank you," I say over my shoulder.

As soon as I'm in the bathroom, I collapse against the door and take a trembling breath. I've never stood up for myself like that before. I feel so out of balance, partially empowered and a little like I want to run back and apologize for being rude. I don't want to push him away, the sex is too good. Insanely good. He wasn't joking when he said he'd ruin me for anyone else.

Pulling my hair back into a messy bun since I don't have time to wash it, I step into the shower. I quickly wash my body and face. It is kind of him to expedite my test results, even with his ulterior motives.

I walk out into the bedroom with my towel wrapped around me to find all my suitcases laid out on the bed. Thomas is dressed in different, slightly nicer, but still casual clothes than before, leaning against the dresser. His eyes rake down me hungrily, his intensity making my stomach do an unwanted flip.

"It's going to be hard to sleep in here with all the bags on the bed like this." I say as I open the suitcase that has all my underwear and pajamas.

"You won't be sleeping in here so it doesn't really matter."

I look up to find his gaze locked on me.

"I don't know. I'm not very tolerant of asshole men anymore. Think I've had my fill."

"I apologized."

"Forgiven, not forgotten," I reply as I pull a matching set of black lace lingerie from my bag.

"Fair enough." He looks out the window for a second before watching me put my panties on with the towel still tucked around me. "Drop the towel. I want to watch you get dressed."

I push my shoulders back and scowl at him. "Who do you think you are?"

"The man you asked to ruin you."

I drop the towel as I put my bra on. "You had your chance."

"That was just the beginning, Siren." He stalks toward me and reaches around to help me clasp my bra. "We do need to restate the ground rules, though."

"Okay, tell me your terms." I step past him and open another suitcase.

"Rule one, this only lasts for a week."

"Agreed," I say as I pull out a pair of jeans.

"Rule two, no feelings or strings."

"Done." I grab a black tank top.

"Rule three, your dad can never find out."

I shoot him a sideways glance. "Obviously."

He nods and watches as I continue to get dressed. "That's what I was struggling with earlier. Thinking about Jack."

"You were thinking about Dad while I was laying naked in your bed?"

"Yes. I was. Thinking about how he'd feel knowing what I had just done to you." He shakes his head and looks back out of the window. "I felt guilty as shit."

"Can you handle the guilt?" I pull my shirt over my head before walking over to him. "Because I won't allow you to take it out on me. I'm dealing with enough fucked up feelings to add yours to the mix."

"I can." He looks down at me and gives me a chaste kiss. "I will. Are you ready? We'll barely make it to the office with enough time."

"I am."

———

THOMAS'S OFFICE is exactly what you'd expect from the best plastic surgeon in Orange County. The space is clean and modern with stylish accents that elevate it from cold and clinical to almost spa-like. He leads me back to a small room with a chair for taking blood samples before poking his head out the door and grabbing an older woman in pink scrubs.

"This is Vanessa," he tells me, "she'll get you taken care of and send you back to my office when you're done." Then he turns his attention to his nurse. "Vanessa, this is my friend's daughter, Brianna. Do you have the orders I sent?"

"Yes, Dr. Brennan. I'll get it all taken care of." She pulls on a pair of latex gloves and sets a few viles out in front of me as he leaves. She goes through a few questions and verifies my identification information before starting.

"How long have you worked for Thomas?" I ask.

I'm curious if he's totally different here. So many plastic surgeons are seeking fame now, but he's managed to stay relatively under the radar, despite having the best practice in the area. Is he truly just a humble man? Do humble surgeons even exist? I've met quite a few who probably couldn't define humility even with the dictionary open to it in front of them.

"I've been here for about eight years." She presses down on my arm, looking for veins.

"What's he like as a doctor?"

"He's an excellent surgeon. Rarely takes time off and has a great bedside manner. All his patients love him as well as his discretion." She cleans my arm. "In fact, we were all surprised when he took today off with such short notice."

Warmth blooms inside me as I realize he took a day off to help me, even before we had sex. It hadn't been planned all along as I assumed. I stop myself from thinking about it too hard, but it really shows that beneath his gruff and cold exterior, there is someone who cares. I want to press her for more information, but I don't want to seem too nosy or thirsty. I don't want there to be whispers in his office for this. It's bad enough he's pulling strings like this at all.

"Quick prick and some pressure," she tells me as she slides the needle in.

She finishes up, hands me a cup, and points me in the

direction of a bathroom. When I finish giving all my samples, she points me down a long hall and tells me his office is at the end. The door is open and a thin blonde with unnaturally large breasts is bent over his desk as they discuss something on the computer. The dress she's wearing is so tight she might as well be naked.

I clear my throat as I enter and they both look up. Thomas smiles and she scowls. I walk over to the desk slowly, giving her a look that says I know exactly what she's trying to do. She looks at me speculatively and then gives me a dismissive smirk. I know it's a mind game, but fuck if it doesn't work just a bit.

"Just a second, Bri." He turns back to his computer. "Clear my schedule for the week except the surgery on Wednesday. I'll be in for that."

"Dr. Brennan," she points at the screen, "you have two other surgeries scheduled this week, too."

"I see that," his tone is snappy as he answers her. "But I also haven't taken a break in sixteen months. I trust you can do your job and get them rescheduled for me, Mindy."

"Of course." She gives him a fake smile and walks out of the office, bumping my shoulder as she goes.

He shuts down his computer and stands, walking over to me. "I cleared my schedule for the week."

"Except for Wednesday?"

He keeps a respectable distance between us as his office door is still open. "Yes, there's a surgery I couldn't push."

"Does some unhappy housewife need an emergency boob job to keep her cheating husband's attention?" I ask playfully.

"No." He gives me an amused look. "I'm doing a cleft palate and lip correction. I volunteer and raise money for a charity that provides treatment for kids born with the condition."

My smug attitude immediately deflates and I feel like a total asshole.

"I'm sorry, Thomas. That is a really incredible thing to do. It was a total dick move for me to make that assumption." I reach down and squeeze his hand.

"Don't worry." He lowers his voice. "I did push a breast augmentation and rhinoplasty back. The sad housewives can wait while I have my fill of you."

His eyes dart over my shoulder and down the hall before coming back to mine.

"And you can pay for that comment while you're on your knees with my cock down your throat tonight."

7

THOMAS

Bri looks so good sitting beside me. The hot sun beats down on her while strands of her hair fly around in the wind. I want to take her home and spend the next thirty or so hours lost inside her, but first we need to grab some dinner.

"Chinese okay?" I ask as we come to a traffic light.

"Yeah." She smiles over at me. "That sounds great."

I set my hand on her thigh, sliding my fingers inside one of the rips in her jeans. Her pleased smile at the move makes my chest warm. It's unimaginable that someone would be stupid enough to sabotage a relationship with her. If Jack wasn't her dad, I'd make her mine in a heartbeat.

I shake that thought from my mind because it's not going to do us any good. Thoughts like that are why I went cold and distant earlier. I was inside her and my inner caveman kept bellowing 'mine, mine, mine.' But she's not mine and she never will be. We just need to let this chemistry between us burn hot and fast. It'll fade out sooner or later.

"Go ahead and order on the app for carry out." I hand her my phone. "Just order me what I have saved under favorites."

"Do you always order the same exact thing?" She looks at me from over the top of her sunglasses with an amused expression.

"I like what I like."

"Rigid," she teases me with a laugh.

"I'll show you rigid tonight," I say as I grab her hand and put it on my crotch.

"It is," she gives my cock a squeeze, "mildly impressive."

"Mildly?"

She giggles and nods. Her laugh is infectious. How have I never realized that before? Not that we ever spent much time together. Maybe a meal here or there over the past few years, but never extended periods of time. It's probably a good thing, considering how attracted to her I am. She pulls her hand away and finishes the order.

We decide to take the food to an overlook where I know there are some picnic tables set up. The wood and metal is worn smooth from use and weathered from the elements. The waves crash against the rocks below and the cool breeze off the Pacific chills our skin.

"Have you decided what you want to do when you graduate? What type of law are you interested in?"

"I'm leaning toward environmental law. With climate change becoming a bigger issue, I know lawsuits will be plentiful. Fighting over resources and access is only going to get worse as the wealth gap increases." She looks out over the coast. "We have to protect this."

I nod in agreement. Building on waterfront land was a huge fucking hassle, but I'm glad it was done properly. Knowing my architect and the coastal coalition triple checked every permit and design eases my mind. The views were worth every setback and headache.

"What about you?" Her voice draws my attention back to her. "Thinking about retirement anytime soon?"

Her eyes sparkle with mischief.

"Can't say that I am." I hold my right hand up. "As long as my hands are steady, I don't think I'll be stopping."

"Seems reasonable."

We banter back and forth for another hour as we watch the sunset. A handful of families and couples pass us going up and down the trail down to the water, but we stay where we are, taking in the surrounding beauty.

"Shall we go home?" I stand and offer my hand.

"Yes," she says, smiling as she slides hers into mine.

I pull her to me, unable to resist the perfection of this moment. A beautiful, intelligent woman in my arms and the sky alight with pink, purple, and orange clouds. Tangling my hands in her hair, I pull her head back and steal a kiss. She opens for me, her tongue sliding against mine in slow, sexy motions that have my dick hardening in my pants.

I said I wasn't going to fuck her again until I could slide inside her bare, but that was a lie. I knew there was no way

I'd be able to show restraint tonight. Not after an evening of easy and deep conversation. And especially not knowing how fucking good she feels.

It's dark by the time we get home and I drag her through the house to my room. Pressing her against the wall, I kiss her. Every kiss has been different, but just as intoxicating as the one that came before. She reaches for my pants, unbuckling my belt first and then pulling my shirt off.

"God, your body is incredible." She runs her hands up and down my abs and chest. "I didn't know this was possible beyond the age of forty."

"Anything is possible if you want it badly enough."

Her eyes hold mine as I make the bold statement, an unreadable look flashing through her eyes. She drops to her knees before me, unzipping my pants. I kick my shoes off as she pulls my pants and boxer briefs off in one go. Her tongue wets her lips as my cock bounces free.

She reaches up and gives me a firm stroke with perfect fucking pressure. Never breaking eye contact, she licks me from base to tip. Fuck, it's sinfully sexy to see the dark desire she has for me in her eyes while she licks my cock like a goddamn porn star.

I reach down and free her hair from the elastic band holding it up. Gathering a fistful, I hold her head in place. I lose all restraint when she says please. Her mouth feels incredible, so hot and wet. She gags when I hit the back of her throat, but I'm not going to ease up on her.

No.

I'm going to fuck her face the way I promised earlier. Ruthlessly, I press all the way down her throat as she struggles to take me. I can already feel my release building. I pull almost all the way out of her mouth, loving the little gasp she makes before slamming back in. As soon as the resistance from her ends and she loosens her jaw I explode down her throat, painting it with hot ropes of cum.

She releases me with a pop and I help her to her feet. A few tears fall from her eyes and I wipe them away with the back of my fingers. Leading her over to the bed I stop her a few feet away.

"I want you to strip for me. Slowly," I tell her.

A brief flash of insecurity crosses her face. "Really?"

"Yes." I frown at her change in demeanor. Gone is the sexy siren swimming naked in my pool and now there's a woman unsure in front of me. "Why?"

She pulls her tank top off and drops it on the floor before answering. "I just feel awkward, knowing that you make people's bodies perfect for a living. When you look at me, I wonder if you're noting my flaws and thinking of how you would fix them." Her eyes dip to the floor as she explains herself.

"Look at me." I wait until her eyes are back on mine. "Your body is a work of art. There is not one thing I would change. Taking a scalpel to you would be a fucking crime against nature." I pull her to me. "I turn at least two women away from my office every week asking for dangerous procedures to get a body like yours."

She shivers under my light touch.

"These curves are dangerous. They were made to make good men do terrible things. Now, step back and strip for me so I can worship at the altar of your body."

She obeys, like a good little siren. Her fingers slowly unbutton her jeans and push them down her hips.

"Turn around for me when you take your panties off."

She hesitates for a moment and then slowly does as I ask. She looks over her shoulder at me as she unhooks her bra and lets it drop beside her. Her eyes stay on mine as she hooks her fingers in the black lace at her hips. She shimmies them down, bending just enough for me to catch a glimpse of her glistening, bare pussy.

"Lay down on the bed, Siren. On your back, in the middle." I instruct.

I watch as she does what I ask before walking to the corner and pulling the attached restraints out. She watches me with curiosity, but no trepidation as I repeat the process on all four sides.

"I'm going to restrain you, is that okay?"

"Yes."

"Have you ever been restrained before?" I do her first wrist.

"No."

I move to her ankles and secure them, petting her pussy as I walk up to finish her other wrist. She shifts in the bed, watching as I pull another condom out of the drawer along with a blindfold and noise canceling headband.

"What are those for?"

"I'm going to take away two of your senses, sight and hearing. Is that okay?"

"Why?"

"Because it will heighten the pleasure of what I'm about to do to you. The only thing you'll be able to concentrate on is the way I'm touching you. It's intensely erotic for both parties."

"You'll stop if I ask you to?"

"Of course, but I don't think you will."

After a slight pause she nods her head. "Okay, I'll try it."

I take her lips in a light kiss.

"My siren is so brave." I put the silk eye mask over her eyes first. "How's that?"

"It feels fine."

"Good. Next is a headband with noise canceling ear pieces. I'll give you a minute to get used to it and then when I squeeze your hand tell me if you're okay."

"Okay," she says as she licks her lips.

I slide the headband around her, moving it over her ears and tucking her hair back. She startles when I run my fingertips down the valley of her breasts. Her breaths are shallow and unsure as she acclimates to the new sensation of sensory deprivation.

I grip her hand and gently squeeze it.

"It's strange, a little disconcerting, but I'm okay."

I reward her by pulling her brown nipple between my lips and gently sucking. Her belly trembles as I lower my hand down, past her cute little innie and over her mound. I keep my mouth on her breasts, switching back and forth to give them equal attention while I tease her with soft strokes everywhere but where she really wants it.

"Thomas," she whimpers as her back arches off the bed. "Please."

I move between her legs and give her pussy a little kiss and her clit a flick of the tongue. Then I plunge my fingers inside her, seeking out her g-spot and circling it until her toes clench and she catches her lip between her teeth. Then I push them even further, searching for her most hidden pleasure center.

"Oh fuck," she exclaims as my fingers sweep over it. "Thomas," she breathes my name like a prayer. "What are you doing?"

I keep going until she's chanting my name over and over, begging for release. I keep the same pace with my fingers, but begin swirling my tongue in circles around her hardened nub. It doesn't take long to get her right to the edge. She cries out my name as she comes, soaking my hand and stubble with the rush of her release.

Her perfect tits rise and fall deeply as she catches her breath.

"Take these off, Thomas."

I oblige and pull the mask and headband off her flushed face. Her eyes immediately find mine and she looks intently at me.

"What did you just do to me?" She wiggles against the restraints.

"Ruined you. Just like you asked."

8

BRIANNA

"Untie me, please, and ruin me with your cock this time."

A wolfish grin splits his face as he reaches up and unbuckles the soft leather restraints on my wrists. He flips me onto my stomach after undoing my ankles. He grips my hips and lifts them, positioning my ass up high. He kneads my thighs and spreads them wide, opening me completely.

"Has anyone had your ass before?" he asks as he lightly teases me there.

"No." The way he pulls pleasure from me makes me think he could probably wring an orgasm out of me just by looking. "But I'm open to it."

"Good." He rewards me by slowly sliding into my pussy.

At this angle, and with how sensitive I still am, I can't stop the moan from falling from my lips. He wraps one hand around my jaw and lifts my head back toward him. The movement pushes him further inside me, where I'm already fluttering with reckless need around his length.

"Look at me." He pulls my head even further back, my neck burning with the stretch. "I'm going to fuck you like you're mine this week. Like I own this beautiful soul and the fucking stunning body that houses it."

"Then do it," I challenge.

I know he was warning me. I know the risk of falling into bed with this man. It's been two days and I already feel more for him than I ever did for the man I was planning to spend my life with. It's twisted and fucked beyond all measure. But right now, in his arms, with his cock buried inside me, I'm ready to burn everything to the ground.

He releases my jaw with a growl and reaches into the still open drawer to pull out a bottle of lube. I feel the cool gel land on my skin and a second later, his finger works inside my ass as he continues to fuck me. The pressure of his finger stretching me while the pace of his cock sliding in and out never falters and has me coming almost immediately.

This orgasm is as deep and powerful as the last he gave me, but the added sensation of my ass being full with his finger adds more pleasure than I thought possible. He's still hard and fucking me with ruthless, deep thrusts. His balls smack me as I lift myself higher for him, an offering of utter depravity as I cry out into the mattress.

He comes with a primal grunt as my name falls from his

lips. He pulls out and collapses to the side of me, his chest rising and falling with exertion.

Every time I think he can't fuck me better than the last time, he does. Each moment with him has me digging a bigger and bigger hole for myself. I have to keep it light, though.

"Not bad for an old man." I manage to keep a straight face. "Did you pop a little blue pill while I wasn't looking?"

He chuckles and my heart beats faster at the sound. I make the mistake of looking over to catch one of his rare smiles. The way his eyes crinkle at the corner and the slight dimple that show make the chip in the wall around my heart worth it.

"You're a brat, you know that?"

"I do my best."

"Do your best and go to sleep, we have a busy schedule tomorrow." He tucks me into his side and pulls the covers over us.

"Doing what?"

"Each other."

I giggle at his deadpan delivery.

"Seriously. I have to be up at four Wednesday morning to be ready for the surgery and the procedures can last all day depending on the case." He kisses my forehead. "That's a whole day of our week gone."

After a quiet moment goes by, I tilt my lips up to his and kiss him. A languid, affectionate kiss that says all the things I can't. His hand moves into my hair as he deepens it, and we lay there in each other's arms, just kissing for what seems like hours when he finally pulls away.

"What was that for?" he asks.

"It is really wonderful what you do. *You* are really wonderful."

Even through the dark of his bedroom, I can feel his gaze burning hot on me. I don't know what he's thinking and he doesn't clue me in. He rolls us so he's tucked against my back, his arms wrapped tightly around me.

―――――

TRUE TO HIS WORD, he fucked me all day Tuesday. In the kitchen, in the bathroom, while we watched a movie in his home theater, and back to the bedroom. I keep wondering when the sex will get boring or repetitive, but so far, so good.

Today, I'm heading up to LA to look at apartments. Last night, while he grilled steaks for dinner, he tossed a set of keys at me. He wants me to look at his house in Venice Beach. It's a long commute for school, but it is far from Trevor's desired neighborhoods. There's a shop there I love for handmade gifts and he would always warn me about being vigilant around the homeless population. No matter how many times I always told him being homeless doesn't equate to being a bad or dangerous person, he would never ease up.

The drive up the coast is nice, I avoid the highway so it takes me longer but I love the beach towns in Orange County. Peeks of the blue water with the sun reflecting off the waves every so often. Kids on playgrounds for the summer. I loved growing up here and if I ever have a family would definitely want to give them similar memories.

By the time I pull up to the house and into the tiny drive attached to the back, it's nearly eleven in the morning. I don't know if I'll take him up on the offer to stay here. He told me to consider it a graduation gift. A quiet, safe place to finish out my last year of law school as I rebuild my life.

I walk to the door and punch the alarm code in as I look around in awe. The space is ultra modern with the black exterior carried over into the inside. The walls are painted black and while it should feel like a cave, it doesn't; it feels open and decadent. There are no walls at the back of the house, only floor to ceiling windows showing the boardwalk and beach beyond.

The kitchen and living room are sparsely furnished. He said he's never spent a night here. He purchased this place more as an investment than anything else. I walk up the open bamboo stairs to the second level where two bedrooms and an office are located. It's a pretty simple floor plan, and the primary suite has the same open windows along the back and a sundeck with several chaise lounges.

People walk and skate past, but it's not too busy being a Wednesday morning. There are a handful of tall palm trees and the wide swath of golden sand before the Pacific takes over the horizon. It is beautiful here. Heading back inside, I'm curious to see what the bathroom is like in this place.

Just like every other room in the house, the walls are black, but the marble on the counter and floor is white with silver veins running through. A chandelier hangs over the stand alone tub with a large shower tucked back in the corner. Two sinks and a lighted vanity stand against the opposite wall.

I can already imagine bringing in tropical plants to liven up the black walls. A California king bed faces out to the ocean and a walk in closet runs the length of the room along the side. I picture some of my belongings scattered through the house. Making dinner in the large kitchen. Drinking wine on the patio with Sara on the weekends.

Then the image of Thomas enters my mind. Him pouring me a glass of champagne, strolling the boardwalk together, going to one of the many little cafes around here. Him fucking me in every room of this house.

I shake my head to get the thoughts out. We're not a thing. We won't be a thing. Can I really accept his gift and live here for a year, rent free, knowing what I'm missing out on?

As if she can hear my thoughts and feel my dilemma, Sara's name flashes against my phone. She's FaceTiming again.

"Hey," I answer the phone as I step out onto the deck.

"Hello, you haven't been answering my calls all week," she says accusatorially. "And where the fuck are you now?"

"Thomas offered to let me stay in one of his investment properties for the next year as a graduation gift." I flip the camera around and show her the back of the house. "It's in Venice, right near the boardwalk."

"Holy shit. I need a tour right now."

I chat with her as I retrace my steps back through the house.

"I'm moving in with you," she says decisively as I show her the kitchen.

I laugh. "I haven't decided if I'm going to take him up on

his offer yet."

"Why not?" She waits for me to flip the camera back to my face. "It's just a gift from your dad's best friend and it makes sense. You tied up a lot of money in your relationship with Trevor. This will help you get back on your feet as you finish school. Win, win, in my opinion."

"It's not that simple." I grimace. If he and I weren't sleeping together, I wouldn't hesitate to graciously accept his offer.

"Why?" she drags out the question. "Wait." Her eyes widen as she realizes. "Is something happening between the two of you?"

I hold eye contact with her as I slowly nod.

"Brianna Lucia." She says my full name with a surprised gasp. "He's twice your age."

"I know."

"And your dad's best friend."

"Yep."

"Is the sex good?"

"The best."

"Fuck." A flurry of emotions cross her face from concern to intrigue to excitement. "I'm glad you're finally getting orgasms."

"So many." I laugh. "I didn't realize half the things he's done to me are possible."

"Well, he is a doctor. Probably has a good handle on anatomy." She goes quiet for a moment. "This is risky, though, and you're on the rebound."

"We have rules," I assure her. "One week only, no feelings, no one can know."

"One of which you've already broken by telling me."

"You don't count."

"Pretty sure he would not say the same."

We stare each other down through the phone.

"The responsible side of me thinks you're playing with fire here," she says, breaking the silence. "But the other part of me wants you to have fun and live a little. Trevor kept you from shining. Right now, you're glowing so bright I don't want to risk you losing it again."

"I know."

A text from Thomas pops up, momentarily distracting me. I tell her I have to go and promise to call her back later. I open his message as soon as we disconnect.

THOMAS: **All your test results came back negative.**

Thomas: **Hope that sweet pussy enjoyed her break because I'm coming for her.**

Me: **Are you done with the surgery?**

Thomas: **Yes, the procedure went well. Are you in Venice?**

I SNAP a quick selfie out on the patio with the beach behind me and send it to him.

THOMAS: **Beautiful**

Thomas: **It suits you**

Me: **Thank you. I'm about to go look at the other**

apartments. I might be late getting home.

Thomas: Do you not like the house?

Me: I love it

Thomas: Then what's the problem?

Me: It's too much. I can't accept it.

Thomas: That's ridiculous. If anything you'd be doing me a favor since I never use it.

Me: I'll think about it

Thomas: We'll talk more about it but start heading home.

Thomas: I have a surprise waiting for you

MY HEART FLUTTERS as I text him that I'm on my way. Why is he sweet, smart, and sexy? Why can't he actually be the cold, arrogant asshole I always thought he was? Is that some defense mechanism he uses to keep people from getting too close? There's got to be a story there.

The man has restraints built into his bed frame, so he clearly has no problem getting laid. I'm sure there is a list a mile long of women waiting for a night with him, but by and large he stays off the radar of the gossip mill. I don't even ever remember him bringing a date around, let alone a girlfriend.

Obviously the easiest way to find out information would be to ask Dad. But that clearly is off the table. There's no way he'd ever be okay with this. He's texted everyday to check in, not just with me, but also with Thomas. I know the guilt after those conversations almost eats him alive.

We can handle this though. Three days down, four to go.

9

THOMAS

The surprise for Bri is a little over the top. Okay, a lot over the top. But she makes me feel. After years of finding nothing but empty one night fucks and pointless conversation, it's like I found my drive again.

I look at her body and I feel desire, want, need.

I could spend hours talking to her about everything and nothing and never get bored.

She's brilliant.

She's beautiful.

She's mine.

But only for four more days, so I'm whisking her away to Mexico where I can go out in public with her on my arm. I'm going to take her out to dinner where I can kiss her, hold her, and dance with her. Where we can let our chemistry and connection out for the world to see.

I already have her bag packed and a jet waiting at the airport to take us down. I called up one of my regular patients yesterday and asked if I could use their house down in Cabo for a few days. They're always offering it up, and if this isn't the perfect opportunity, I don't know what is.

There are perks to being a plastic surgeon to the ultra wealthy, and this is definitely one of them. While some of my colleagues chase fame on the internet and television, I welcome discretion, and clients who don't want their name and procedures accidentally leaked to the press.

My leg bounces as I hear the garage door open and Brianna's footsteps down the hall. Her wide smile when she sees me is all I need. My God, she's gorgeous. It's only been twelve hours since we've seen each other, but my eyes drink in the sight of her in a pair of cut off denim shorts and an olive green tank top, like I haven't seen her in days. Her raven locks flow over her shoulder, just begging for my fingers.

"What's this?" She points at the two suitcases and looks at me quizzically.

"Feel like getting away for a few days?"

"Where to?"

"Mexico." I grab her wrist and pull her between my legs. "One of my patients has a house they're always offering up. I called yesterday to see if it was available. It is and I have a jet on standby to take us there now."

"Really?" She steps back and looks at me. "Just like that?"

"Just like that. Let me spoil you out in the open for a few days."

I can see the indecision warring on her face. It probably feels like a lot. First the house. Now a trip. But I want this and she'll enjoy it so I stand and link our fingers together. She follows, but I can feel the hesitancy in every step.

By the time we're climbing the steps to the plane she's much more on board with the trip idea. I know she's flown private before, her father is the CEO of an investment firm, they have money. She just isn't interested in living life on her dad's dollar. I've always known that. Jack complains all the time about how she refuses his money, aside from school. She still drives the Audi he got her when she graduated from high school.

Brianna settles into one of the oversized chairs and accepts a glass of champagne from the flight attendant, her long, bare legs crossing as she looks out the window.

She takes a sip and then looks over at me. "I don't think I can accept the house."

"I'm not giving it to you," I scoff. "I'm letting you live there for a year as a graduation gift."

"It's got to be a ten million dollar property." She takes another sip. "It's too much for what this is." She gestures back and forth between us.

"What is this?" I challenge her. This is a dangerous game, poking at each other for labels and definitions. It goes against the very rules I set down. But I want her to push. If she pushes, I push back. I'll meet her and face the repercussions together.

"A one week sex fest." She leans toward me. "I gave you

my body for one week."

"Yes." I lean forward, too, nose to nose. "You begged me to ruin you. Let. Me."

"Sexually. Not emotionally. Not mentally." Her eyes lock on mine. "I won't be paid off like some high class whore."

Her words shock me into silence. Have I made her feel like that? Surely not. I don't know where this is coming from.

"You are so far from being a whore." I take her glass and set it down, gripping her fingers in my hands. "I just want to make sure you are taken care of."

"Yeah, well." She pulls her hands away. "I have a dad for that."

"Don't fucking remind me," I growl. Bile swirls in my stomach.

"Maybe you need the reminder. We're not permanent. We can't be. Which is why I am so grateful for this trip and the offer of the house, but come Sunday night, we're walking away from each other."

She's not wrong. It was always the agreement. But why does my chest ache at the thought? This is a feeling I've not felt for so long.

"I'm sorry for bringing this up right now." She unclips her seat belt and crawls into my lap. "I want to spend the next few days enjoying each other. I appreciate everything you've done so much."

She leans down and kisses my neck, her tongue darting out with quick little licks. Her hips rock against me and my dick takes over. I pull her tank top over her head and squeeze her tits, obsessed with how soft they are filling my hands. She groans at the rough treatment. My little siren has a subtle kinky side. Given enough time, I'm sure I could have her doing all sorts of depraved shit.

Her shorts are loose enough that I can reach up and pull them to the side. My dick aches for her as I slide my fingers into her tight cunt, already finding it soaked and ready for me. Her fingers work the zipper of my pants when I slide my thumb over her clit.

"Fuck," she whispers against my lips as I use my fingers to ready her.

I haven't been inside her without a condom yet, but now we know it's safe. I wanted to wait until I could fully enjoy the experience, but desperate times call for desperate measures. An angry fuck is what we both need right now. As soon as my cock is free of my pants I thrust inside her, my grip on her hips so tight my knuckles turn white. She feels incredible, hot, wet, tight. She feels like home.

"Ride me," I command. "Hate fuck me because you already know you're falling for me."

Her hands move down to my shoulders as she moves up and down my cock fluidly. I pull the cups of her bra down so I can see her tits and bite down on one of the brownish-pink buds, which only spurs her to go harder.

"Come loud enough for the flight crew to hear. Let them all know it's just a week long fuck fest." I know I'm being an ass, throwing her harsh words back at her like this, but it doesn't stop me.

I feel her walls tighten around me and let myself go before she gets to her climax. As I surge inside her, finally filling her, I pull her head back by the hair and bite down on her neck. She'll probably have a mark, but I don't care. At least she'll be marked as mine for a little while.

Her pussy spasms around me as she comes, her movements slowing as her breathing deepens. She collapses into my arms, her head tucked on my shoulder.

"I'm sorry," I whisper into her ear.

She just shakes her head in response.

THE REMAINDER of the flight and the drive to villa are long and silent. She spent most of the time reading a book on her phone or texting her friend. Occasionally her lips would curl up in a smirk at something that came through, but she never flashed that gorgeous smile at me.

"Wow," she says as she walks through the open living area and out onto the patio. "This place is incredible."

"It is."

The backyard has a large kidney shaped pool with towering palm trees marking the property line from the sandy beach beyond. A cabana that looks more like a four poster bed with linen canopies stands to one side while an outdoor kitchen and chairs claims the others. The entire house is open to the views in the back, either through windows or folding glass doors.

I wrap my fingers around her dainty wrist and pull her back against me. "Are you still mad at me?"

"No." She leans back against me, tilting her head to give me better access as I nibble her earlobe. "I just don't want to accept handouts. From anybody, not just you." I'm not happy with that and I want to press the issue. But now isn't the time. I'll wait to bring it up when she's not so overwhelmed.

"Okay." I kiss her neck and wrap my arms around her waist. "We'll table it for now. The owner is sending her private chef to prepare our dinner tonight. Let's just enjoy our time down here together."

"Agreed." She turns in my arms and sinks her fingers in my hair. "I'm going to go take a shower and see what you packed for me."

I claim her mouth with mine, tempted to strip her down right here. Her sinful taste consumes me as her tongue glides along my own. I love feeling her soft, full lips. Ending our kisses is the hardest thing I've ever done, but I need to make a few calls to check on patients and return some emails.

I smack her ass after we break apart. "I have a little work to do; I'll find you in a bit."

I watch as she prances off into the house, and then take a seat on one of the lounge chairs, pulling my phone out. The first notification I see is a missed call from Jack. My stomach sours as I listen to his voicemail asking about Bri and thanking me yet again for taking such good care of her.

If he knew my version of taking care of her was fucking her on every available surface, I think his feelings would be very different. He and Bri are so close. They have been since the day his wife's casket was lowered into the ground. I know this would forever change my friendship with him, but the last thing I want to come from this is a wedge driven between them.

This just hardens my resolve to end things on schedule, keeping to the rules. I know I'm already developing real feelings for her and sometimes the way she looks at me makes me think she could, too. But we have to keep fighting those feelings. For us. For Jack.

I send Jack a text back telling him that everything is great and that Bri is doing well. Both of which are true.

I spend another twenty minutes looking through notes and emails about the patients my colleagues have been providing care for during my time off. When I'm sure that I've seen everything of the highest importance, I sign out and text the office manager that I'll be completely out of touch until Saturday.

The chef has already finished dinner and shown me where it's being kept warm before I walk through the house in search of Bri. She's fixing her hair when I find her. Her eyes meet mine in the mirror as I step into the bathroom.

"You're a devilish man, you know that?" She smirks at me.

"Why?" I ask with feigned innocence.

"No panties. You packed everything I needed, but forgot underwear."

"I guess you don't need them, then."

I run my hand down the soft, green cotton of the dress she's wearing, over the curve of her hip. I'm glad I packed this one at the last minute. With her deeply tan skin and killer fucking body, this dress looks perfect. She is perfect.

10

BRIANNA

Thomas grabs my hand and leads me back through the house. Mischief sparkles in his green eyes as he looks over his shoulder at me. He looks so young and carefree at this moment, I wish I had a camera to capture it.

If I had my phone, I would try to sneak a photo. But before I took a shower, I checked my messages and saw at least a dozen texts from an unknown number. When I checked them, I realized they were all from Trevor. I blocked the new number, sent Dad and Sara check in messages, then turned off my phone. I want this trip to be about relaxing and feeling good.

Guilt from lying to my dad will eventually come. I just want to live in the moment. Sara can talk some sense into me later on, but right now I'm just going where life takes me. And as for Trevor, I don't know. I don't miss him. I don't really even hurt. I just want him gone from my life.

"What are you thinking about up there?" I don't even realize Thomas has stopped until he taps my temple, looking down at me.

"How I don't want to think while we're down here. I just want to live in the moment and feel."

"Feel what?" he asks as he cups my cheek with hooded eyes.

"You. Us." I swallow as his thumb glides over my lips. "Whatever this insane chemistry is between us."

"Good answer."

His lips take mine in a slow, sensual kiss and I gasp when he slides his fingers back into my hair and pulls at the roots, tilting my head back for an even deeper angle. Heat builds in my core as he breaks from my lips and begins kissing down my neck.

I begin unbuttoning his shirt, whimpering at the sharp bite of his teeth against my sensitive flesh. He unties the straps of my dress, my breasts falling free from the cotton that was supporting them. His skin is hot and smooth as I run my fingers up his torso to push the shirt off his wide shoulders.

"Turn around. Face down on the table, Siren." He pushes me down gently. "I'm going to show you how the devil takes his dinner."

He runs his fingers up the back of my legs, pushing my dress over my hips. With his foot, he moves each of mine out wide, hooking them both around opposite legs of the table.

The muscles in my legs burn at the stretch. The marble table top is cold against my cheek and breasts.

He kneads my ass cheeks, spreading me apart in the most embarrassingly sexy way. Everything is on display for him right now as he lets his eyes feast on my body.

He runs a finger through my folds softly, teasingly. "You're already soaked, Siren, and I've barely touched you."

He slides a finger inside me, gently stroking my front wall. I arch my back, wanting more, but he quickly removes his hands.

"I'm in charge. You lay there like a good girl and don't move." He circles my clit, his finger wet from my juices. "I'll reward you with all the orgasms your body can handle before crumbling into an exhausted mess at my feet."

"Yes," my voice comes out as a breathy whisper.

"Good girl."

He slides two fingers back inside me, pumping them in and out torturously slow, and I whimper every time his fingers slide over my g-spot. Then his thumb runs over the sensitive skin between the entrance of my ass.

I hear him drop to his knees behind me and as his hands move from inside me to squeeze my hips and open me even further, it takes all my willpower not to arch my back and beg for his tongue.

Luckily, it never comes to that because I feel his breath on my parted folds as he licks up one side and down the other. He moans against me as his tongue glides back and forth over my clit and I grip my hands around the edge of the table to keep from grinding back against his face.

"Fuck, my siren tastes so sweet." He pulls my bundle of

nerves between his lips and sucks, making me cry out in pleasure.

"Oh, Thomas." I cry out as his tongue moves to my pussy. "Fuck. Please." I moan, my knuckles turning white as I hold myself still.

"Please what?" he taunts.

"Please make me come."

I feel him smile against me as he keeps licking and sucking and rubbing every sensitive part of me. Then I feel his fingers slide past my g-spot, all the way deep inside me. He starts the same back and forth motion as I feel my release building again. Pressure and pleasure build as he keeps his mouth on my clit and his fingers inside me.

"Do you know what this is?" He pulls back for a second. "It's called your a-spot."

I don't give a fuck what it's called as long as he keeps making me cum like this. My toes curl as I orgasm with a silent scream. My walls clamp tight around his fingers as I flood him with my arousal. I collapse from the inside out, trembling through wave after wave of powerful release and I can feel myself dripping down my thighs. My nipples ache against the cold marble.

Thomas stands and smacks my ass. "Roll over and sit on the edge of the table."

I eagerly comply.

He grabs my feet and places them on each corner, so my legs are bent and spread completely open. I lean back on my hands watching him as he lowers his zipper and takes his cock out. He steps between my legs and drags the head of his cock through my folds while staring into my eyes.

"I want you to watch me enter you, Bri." He positions himself at my entrance. "I want you to feel and see every inch of me own every inch of you."

I watch as he slowly disappears inside me, feeling the stretch of my walls around his thick length. His cock twitches as he pushes fully inside. He pauses and then slowly slides back out. Then moves in again with the same achingly slow pace. It feels like he wants to stake his claim on every single part of me.

He slams into me ruthlessly hard with a growl. "Mine."

My face jerks up to his, my brown eyes meeting his green as something snaps inside him. I can feel the primal pull of our connection stretch taut between us. His control is gone with the last of the dying sunlight and I nod at him as he thrusts into me again with another growled *mine*.

His abs ripple with power as he moves in and out of me and he reaches down to pinch my clit as he holds off his own release. Grabbing me by the back of the neck, he pulls me to him for another kiss and I moan his name against his lips as my pleasure peaks once more. He greedily gulps down my panted moans as he fills me with his release, his cock jerking inside me as he marks me with his cum.

Resting his forehead against mine, we both catch our breath. When he pulls out of me after a brief kiss, he commands me to stay where I'm at. He disappears into the kitchen and comes back a moment later with a damp cloth that he uses to clean me up with. I slide off the table when he finishes and retie the straps on my dress before excusing myself to the bathroom.

My breaths are erratic as I look at my reflection in the

mirror. I look well and truly freshly fucked. My hair is a mess. My nipples are still hard and poking through my dress. A bite mark mars the skin of my neck. All of that pales in comparison to how fucked I truly am on the inside.

He claimed me with each thrust, each growled *'mine'*. This is insanity. Five days ago, I was engaged to another man. Now I'm here, in Mexico, fucking my dad's best friend. I should run. I should sneak out in the night.

I sure as fuck should not feel like this is right. Every time he said 'mine', I nodded at him in agreement. As if my body was calling the shots. Just because the guy is a good fuck does not mean I'm his. I've never had a guy claim me like that while fucking me. I shouldn't even want it. It's wrong.

The rules.

We're breaking the rules.

With deep breaths and a splash of cold water to my face, I remind myself what they are. I can go back out there and enjoy dinner and his company without falling in love with him. I just have to remember.

It's not love. It's lust.

Simple.

When I walk back out onto the patio, Thomas is pouring glasses of what looks like margaritas for us. His shirt is back on and you would never know by looking at him that he just fucked me like a madman five minutes ago. His pupils flare when he notices the mark on my neck. He looks pleased as he takes in my appearance, so different from his.

"The chef left dinner warming in the oven. I'll go grab it."

He walks back into the house and I take a seat at the

table, admiring the small arrangement of tropical flowers and candles in the center. A few birds calling and the waves in the background are the only sounds I can hear. It's completely dark now, the moon nearly full.

"The plates are hot; be careful." Thomas sets one down in front of me first and then serves himself. The sizzling steak and fragrant chimichurri sauce have my mouth watering. We eat quietly for a few minutes, both of us taking in the ambiance around us.

"Did you ever want to get married or have kids?" I ask as I take a sip of my drink. "Or was it always the bachelor life for you?"

He looks up at me in surprise as he finishes chewing his bite. "I was married, actually. Right between college and medical school."

"Oh." I let that brand new bit of information process. "What happened?"

He sighs and sets his fork down before taking a drink. "She was coming home from one of her rounds as a resident and was hit by a drunk driver. Killed instantly." A melancholic gaze takes over his features, as if he's picturing her inside his head.

"I'm so sorry." Tears prick my eyes. "Forget I asked something so rude."

"It's not rude to ask those types of questions to the person you're sleeping with. I don't mind talking about her. It's been a while."

"Tell me about her if you want."

"Her name was Janet. She was gorgeous, in a studious way. Always wore her hair back and had these sexy glasses."

He smiles fondly at the memory. "We had several courses together, both of us being pre-med, and after a year or so of getting to know her, I asked her out."

He pauses to take another drink and looks out over the glassy surface of the Pacific. "I proposed during our senior year of college and we got married the weekend after we graduated. She loved kids and was planning on opening her own pediatric practice eventually."

"She sounds amazing," I say softly.

"She was," he quietly agrees. "She was twelve weeks pregnant with what would have been our first baby."

His eyes glitter with unshed tears as my heart shatters for him and I reach across the table and cover his hand with mine.

"Thomas," I whisper. "I am so sorry."

He gives me a bittersweet smile as he links our fingers.

"I'm surprised that in all the years I've known your dad this hasn't come up before. I actually met him in a round-about way because of that." He scoots his chair back and pats his knee.

I waste no time moving to his lap and sliding my fingers into his hair. "Because you're both widowers?"

"Yeah, but actually, we met because of your mom."

My brow furrows, I don't remember ever meeting Thomas until after she died. "Really?"

"She had a friend who was going through breast cancer treatments at the same time she was battling pancreatic cancer. I did her friend's breast augmentation after her mastectomy. Somehow those two got to talking about my wife passing away."

"And Mom knew she wasn't going to make it." I nod, catching onto where this is going.

"Yeah, even fifteen years later, pancreatic cancer is still one of the most deadly forms. She knew the likelihood of her not surviving and reached out to me. She essentially made Jack and I into our very own support group for each other."

A hot tear rolls down my cheek. It was so like my mom to try to take care of us from beyond the grave.

He catches the next tear with his thumb. "She told me she wanted Jack to have someone who understood his pain after she was gone. Luckily for us, we became fast friends beyond the shared grief of two men losing their wives far too soon."

A sob rips from my chest as grief comes tearing from me. The love that my parents had for each other was so palpable that I could feel it, even as a child. There was never any doubt that they were it for each other.

I can't stop the tears now that they've started. I cry because I miss my mom so much. Sometimes I walk into her closet and bury my face in her dresses, hoping that her scent will still be there all these years later. It always is because Dad periodically sprays her perfume on them. I miss the look I'd catch in my dad's eyes as he would watch Mom cook dinner, dancing around the kitchen to cheesy eighties love songs.

Tears fall for my dad who had the love of his life, but knew he was going to lose her. I sob for Thomas who lost his wife and baby with no warning, no time to prepare. The absolute terror that Janet had to have died with, even if only for a split second. It's not fair. So much death and tragedy for two families to have to bear. I can feel Thomas's shuddering breaths against me as he struggles to hold himself together while I fall apart in his lap.

Grief is like a river, though. You can stone wall it for days, months, years, but one rock comes loose and all of it bursts free. I'm the queen of building walls around my grief, and now, safe in his arms, it's all coming free. I cry onto his shoulder for so long and so hard I eventually fall asleep.

I wake briefly as he jostles me into his arms and carries me back inside the house. Through the haze of emotional exhaustion, I feel my dress come off and his hot body slide into bed behind me. His arms wrap around me and hold me close the rest of the night.

11

THOMAS

I did not think opening up about Janet last night was going to have the effect it did on Brianna. Watching her heart break open like that was the most painful thing I have ever experienced. That isn't hyperbole, it was harder to hold her through her pain than it ever was to feel my own.

I'm shaken today. Shaken because I feel something for Bri I've never felt before. I loved Janet with all my heart. She was my best friend, my partner and I have no doubt that I would still be happily married to her today.

But Bri makes me want to go to war for her. I want to destroy anything that makes her sad. I want to protect her from pain. I want to own her body and heart. These feelings are damn near barbaric in their intensity.

It's nearly noon and she's still sleeping. I keep wandering in to check on her every hour or so. At least that's the lie I tell myself. I'm actually just obsessed with watching her while her guard is down. Her expression in sleep is so soft and she looks so insanely young, even though she's well into adulthood.

A couple of strands of her silky, raven hair have fallen over her forehead. Her plump lips are slightly parted, daring me to kiss her until she comes alive underneath me. Deciding that's exactly what I need to do, I gently pull the sheet down her body, exposing one inch of flawless, golden skin at a time.

She rolls from her side onto her back, one thigh falling open allowing for a perfect opportunity for me. I strip my clothes off because it feels like a crime to not be naked with this woman. Laying down beside her I run my fingers over her soft belly. Her curves are the sweetest temptation. I love looking at her like this, relaxed and natural, not trying to hold her body in a way to make herself look different.

Her back arches as I wrap my lips around one of her pert nipples. I run my finger in teasing strokes over her slit. She's going to be writhing beneath me with need before she's even fully awake.

It doesn't take much to get her wet, her body is so incredibly responsive to touch. I move my mouth from one nipple to the other and her hips begin grinding into my hand. She moans as I slide a finger between her folds, circling her clit with the same pressure as my tongue on her nipple.

She slides her fingers through my hair in a way that's become entirely too familiar over the past few days. My name tumbles from her lips as I pump two fingers inside her, curling them up against her g-spot. Her hand wraps around my cock and tugs.

I let her work me until I'm hard and she's ready. Our lips meet for a lazy kiss as I shift my weight and settle between her thighs, then her legs wrap around my waist as I slide deep inside her. Her heels dig into my ass as we find a perfect rhythm with each other she clings to me, working her clit while I rock in and out of her pussy. Her walls flutter around my cock as she comes, and she says my name over and over with each wave of her orgasm, the sound of her heady voice sending me over the edge.

But I don't cum inside her this time. In a moment of pure possessiveness I pull out and cum over her belly. Thick ropes of my hot release land across her stomach. I know I scared her when I told her she was mine last night so this is the next best thing.

She looks down at her belly, her lips parted in surprise, then her honey brown eyes look up at mine and I see the unspoken understanding in them. She's not ready to admit this is something more than a week long tryst, but I am. With every passing moment, I know deeper and deeper down that she is mine. I use my hand to rub myself into her skin as she watches me with bated breath.

It started off physically, but then there's the hours of conversation, her wit and intelligence leaving me captivated. Last night sealed the deal for me. She opened up in a way I know, without words, that she doesn't do with many people. I'm not even sure she's let Jack see that raw, hurting, loving side shine through. Now that I have, it will not be easy to let go of.

I lay down beside her and she immediately curls onto her side. She fits against me perfectly. Her fingers run through the light dusting of hair on my chest.

"What are we doing today?" she asks as she stretches against me.

"I thought we could go into town. Maybe do some shopping and then grab dinner."

"That sounds amazing." Her small hand cups my cheek and turns my face away from the view out the window and back to her. "That was the best wake up call I've ever had."

"Good." I almost slip up and tell her to get used to it. Luckily I realize just in time to stop myself. I kiss her instead.

"I'll go take a shower." She looks over her shoulder as she saunters toward the bathroom at me. "Do you want to join me?"

I'm out of the bed and behind her in seconds.

"Gracias," Bri tells the owner of a boutique jewelry store as we exit. I'm coming back at some point to purchase the necklace she kept eyeing, but I want to surprise her with it on our last night together.

"I didn't realize you were fluent in Spanish." I lead her through a small crowd gathered around a street performer.

"Yes, it was honestly harder than I thought it would be to learn in college. Mom spoke Portuguese to me as much as

Dad spoke English so I grew up bilingual. But the two languages are surprisingly different. No offense, but I'm surprised at how fluent you are."

I shrug. "Growing up in southern California will do that to you."

"I grew up in the same place and plenty of people around me never cared to learn another language." She raises her eyebrows at me.

"My childhood best friend's parents were migrant workers. I spent as much time with him and his family as I did my own. It rubs off when you're getting yelled at in a different language."

"Where are you from?" she asks with a frown. "I never thought to ask before."

"Outside of San Diego." I lean in to whisper in her ear. "And you never thought to ask because we were never fucking before."

She playfully shoves me away as we keep walking along the marina and chatting. She points out a little restaurant with a deck overlooking the water and suggests dinner there. We end up at a perfect table, overlooking the water and watching sailboats and yachts go by.

"That seems fun." She points at a catamaran cutting through the water. "I've always wanted to spend a day laying on the deck of one of those."

We chat for a few more minutes before the server comes to take our drink order. When Bri excuses her to use the restroom I call the server back over and ask for the best catamaran tour company. She rattles off a few names and I call the first I see with a high rating. Before Bri is even back from the restroom, I've reserved a private tour for tomorrow. It probably cost three times what it normally would have, being so last minute, but a black card talks more than a hundred gold cards do.

"I think it's going to be hard to walk away from this," Bri says as we're finishing our after dinner drinks.

"Mexico?"

"No." She gives me a sassy side eye. "Us."

"Do we have to walk away?" I ask cautiously.

"Yes. Dad would flip his shit and you know it."

She's not wrong. But this feels so right.

"What if we extended the terms? Maybe the entire summer until you go back to school?"

"I can't live in your house for the summer."

"Maybe not my Palos Verdes house, but you could live in my Venice Beach house. If you just accept the gift, I could spend the weekends with you."

Visions of us together in that house fill my head. Taking walks up and down the boardwalk. Finding all the little hidden gems tucked in the neighborhood. Saturday mornings at the farmers market and lazy Sunday mornings in bed.

"Thomas." She sighs. "I can't. I can't be your kept woman."

"Fine. I'll have a rental contract drawn up and you can pay me rent." I'll make it one dollar, but it'll still be contractually sound.

"I'm sure you'd have me underpaying."

"Absolutely I would. But guess what? I have more money than I'll ever be able to spend on my own. I could quit working today and still afford my current lifestyle. Money isn't an issue for me so why don't you let me take care of you in whatever way I can?"

"Because you're not my boyfriend. You're not my fiancé or husband. Even then, I wouldn't feel right just spending all your money frivolously." She tosses back the rest of her margarita and stands, dropping her napkin on the table. "We're just a fling."

We both stew in anger on the way back to the house. As soon as the front door closes behind us, I push her against the wall with my body. Her eyes flash with anger even as her pelvis rubs against mine, seeking some way to ease the ache I know she feels without me inside her.

"Since we're just a fling, you won't mind me fucking you like one, will you?" I challenge her.

Her eyes bounce back and forth between mine as she grits out, "Do your worst."

I push her down to her knees before she even finishes. My cock throbs against the metal bite of the zipper holding it back from the warmth of her mouth. She tears my pants open and yanks me out, roughly running her fist over my length.

I push past her lips as soon as they part, wincing at the dark pleasure of her teeth scraping against me. If my siren wants it rough, I'll fucking give it to her rough. I stop her movements around me by gripping both sides of her face.

"Relax your jaw," I command.

As soon as I feel her facial muscles go lax, I begin ruthlessly fucking her face. Every gag she makes around me brings me closer to nirvana. One of her hands grips my thigh while the other moves between her legs. My girl is getting herself off to this and it drives me fucking feral. I thrust against her so hard tears run down her cheeks and her head hits the wall behind her. Her hand moves faster under her dress as she cries out around my cock shoved down her throat.

The vibration of her moan sends me over the edge and I pull out of her just before I come. "Show me your tongue."

She dutifully complies and I shoot my cum into her mouth, over her tongue, and across her face. She looks into my eyes the entire time. When the last shot lands on her face I tuck my cock back in my pants and rub my finger over the mess I made. Pushing it all into her mouth.

"Swallow."

I watch as she does and then walk out the back door and to the pool.

12

BRIANNA

H e's mad and I'm confused. That was the most degrading thing I've ever done and I would sign up to do it a million more times. I watch as he strides away, peeling his clothes off one item at a time before diving naked into the pool.

I take slow steps out to the patio unable to decide if I should get in with him or leave him alone. I can feel the turmoil radiating off him. I decide to strip and dive in with him. After all, I'm the reason he's upset in the first place.

Swimming over to him, the water cools me with every stroke, but instead of taking a space beside him, I wrap my arms around his waist and press a kiss to his spine. He lowers his arm and covers mine with his before reaching around and dragging me in front of him.

"I'm sorry. That was out of line." He kisses my forehead. "Is your head okay from hitting the wall?"

"My head hit the wall?" I ask. I honestly don't remember and nothing hurts.

"Yes. While I was fucking that sassy mouth of yours."

"Didn't feel it." I wrap my arms around his shoulders. "I'm fine."

"I'm not." He pulls me closer. "I was like an animal in there."

"A big raging one." I bite down on his lip. "I fucking loved it."

His eyes fly to mine. "You did?"

I nod. "No one has made me come like you do. Every time we're together, it's better and newer and unique to the last time. I literally never know what I'm going to get from you."

"I do have quite a few tricks up my sleeve." He smirks down at me.

"I want to learn them all," I tell him, realizing that I do, in fact. Even if it takes years. And that thought makes unease rise within me. Because at the end of the day, what we want and what we can feasibly have, are two very different things. He must sense my train of thought because while he doesn't let go of me, he does break eye contact.

"I'll give you as much as I can in the time that we have," he says, his voice laden with resignation.

I wrap my legs around his waist and my arms around his neck before kissing him. "That's all we can do for each other, isn't it?"

He glides around the pool with me attached to him, his

hands wandering over my body. He's so familiar with it that he can work me right up to the edge and then back away. All the while we talk about life, his goals. My goals. The next investment property he has his eye on, a cabin in Aspen.

"What's the plan for tomorrow?" I ask when the conversation comes full circle to the present.

"A surprise." he grins at me, a dimple popping out.

"I love surprises."

"You're definitely going to love this one. All you need is a bikini and some sunscreen."

He kisses me and swims us over to the steps. "I'll go grab us some towels. You wait here." He gives me another kiss.

I watch him walk away, his ass still high and tight. "You've got a hot ass for an old man," I yell.

He grins over his shoulder at me and heat burns through my chest, making it feel like it's constricting. He's so sexy it takes my breath away.

THE NEXT MORNING I'm looking at the two bikinis he packed for me, mildly annoyed that I only have two to choose from, when Thomas walks into the bedroom.

"What are you doing? The car will be here in five minutes."

"Which one should I wear?" I motion back and forth between the two.

"Uh." He looks between me and the bed. "Does it really matter? They're both bikinis, right?"

"One covers significantly more than the other."

"Go with less coverage." He winks at me. "Definitely." His phone buzzes with a notification. He glances down quickly to read the message and then back up at me. "Put it on, cover up, grab your stuff, and let's go. The car's out front."

He leaves the room as I pull the black bikini on. The bottoms are a thong that sits high up on my hips, barely covering my front either. The top is a plunge bra top with just enough support to keep me from being obscene. I grab the white sarong I bought yesterday and wrap it around my hips and toss a tank over my head. After a cursory glance in the mirror to make sure nothing is hanging out, I meet him by the front door.

He's been acting weird and smug all morning so I have no idea what to expect today. The car drives past the town shopping area and resorts toward the marina. He pulls me from the car and down the dock to a gleaming white cata-maran. It looks like one of the ones we saw last night with dozens of people milling around, but this one is empty aside from four crew members.

"Thomas." I look over at him in awe. "How did you do this on such short notice?"

"A couple calls and a few swipes of my credit card is all it took."

He steadies me as I step from the dock to the boat. A crew member hands me a frozen tropical drink as I look around in wide-eyed wonder. Thomas takes his drink and links our fingers together as they show us around the boat. There's a bar and covered seating area with large cushions and gorgeous tropical floral arrangements everywhere. They show us the deck with a few benches nailed down. Then there's the spot I've always dreamed of laying out on, the net that is open to the sea below. A few outdoor cushions and pillows are tossed down for comfort.

I ask if I can lay out on that now and the crew member giving the tour gives me the okay. I strip my top and sarong off, stuffing them into the straw bag I bought. Thomas sucks a breath through his teeth as his eyes sear a path up my body.

"I definitely told you to choose the wrong suit." His voice is strained as he steps between me and the rest of the crew.

"You wanted less coverage." I get down and crawl across the net, making damn sure I give Thomas the full effect of these bottoms. "You got less coverage."

He pulls his shirt over his head and lays out beside me. "I'm going to make you pay for this torture later tonight."

"I'm looking forward to that."

I pull his face down to mine for a kiss and he rolls onto his side, blocking me from view as his hands roam over my curves. Occasionally, they dip below the material of my bikini, teasing a nipple or running under the hem of my bottoms.

"If you don't stop that I'm going to slide on top of you and fuck you in front of the crew." I bite down on his lip. "You're kinky, but I feel like you wouldn't want to share that moment with strangers."

"I made you cum on camera for your ex to see." His fingers dive between my folds. "God, that was so fucking hot.

Feeling this cunt dripping for me as you came apart in my arms. He's lucky I didn't strip you down right there and fuck you for him. I bet he was hard, watching."

His dirty talk and deft fingers have me grinding against his hand with heaving breaths. "Feel how wet you are? Just thinking about what a dirty girl my siren is makes you hot."

The boat hits a wave and my tummy flips deliciously. His fingers dip deep inside me in the way only he can do, rubbing back and forth. I should care about the fact that the crew can probably tell what we're doing but I don't. He makes me want to be an exhibitionist.

"Fuck," I cry out as we hit another wave. The sensation of the boat along with his fingers has me spasming around him. He kisses me through my panted cries, too possessive to let anyone else hear me come.

"Clean your mess," he holds his fingers to my lips and I lick them as he slides them into my mouth. I love the way I taste on his skin. I hollow my cheeks and look into his eyes as he withdraws them. "Fucking perfect," he whispers before kissing me again.

The rest of the day goes by entirely too fast. The catered lunch is delicious and the drinks never stop flowing. We take a tandem kayak around the Arch of Cabo San Lucas, stopping at Lovers Beach, and as we go back to port in the evening, a pod of dolphins plays in our wake. It was the most perfect day he could have given me. It was the most perfect trip he could have given me, actually.

Even though we've had disagreements, it's only because we both have feelings developing. It's hard to handle the duality of our situations. No one sees me as clearly as he does, just as no one is as forbidden as he is. This was always a losing game.

The sun is setting as we get home so we decide to make the most of it. The waves roll over our feet as we walk hand in hand through the foamy surf. As if by some unspoken agreement, we just walk, enjoying the last dying rays of the sun. We only have tonight here and tomorrow night back in California together and I'm determined not to get in another argument.

"I have something for you. Just a little gift." He pulls a long jewelry box wrapped with a bow out of his pocket and hands it to me.

"Thomas," I trail off. "You didn't have to do this."

"I know. I wanted to." He nudges my shoulder with his. "Open it."

I untie the ribbon and open the box, seeing the necklace I was eyeing at the boutique inside. It's even more beautiful in the pinkish purple light of the sunset. An opal with tiny pavè diamonds surrounding it. It's stunning.

"Will you put it on me?" I ask.

"Of course." He takes the delicate chain and loops it around my neck, clasping it with ease. "It's beautiful."

"It is." I rise onto my toes and kiss him. "Thank you. Opal was my mom's birthstone."

He wraps his arms around me and holds me. On the rare occasions I would let down my emotional guard and be vulnerable with Trevor, he never did this. He would give me a brief hug and then move onto whatever else was on his agenda. It feels like Thomas would hold me forever if I needed him to.

"Let's head back to the house," he says as he lets me go. "We have to take an early flight since it was such a last minute trip."

13

THOMAS

Brianna is curled up in the chair across from me as I go through the emails I've been neglecting. Her headphones are on and her eyes are shut as she catches a little more sleep and the flight attendant comes by and tucks a blanket around her and brings me a cup of coffee.

Luckily, I get most of my work done on the plane; that way when we get back to my house this morning, I can spend the rest of the day and night inside her. I want to soak up as much time with her in my house as I can. I've been wracking my brain trying to figure out a way to get her to let me rent my house to her. It is the best way for us to be together. The only way, really.

I'm not ready to let her go.

It feels like time is speeding by faster and faster the sooner we get to our expiration date. I finish my work right as the plane touches down, which is good, but still a reminder that we have maybe twenty-four hours left. I wake her with a kiss, and my heart flip flops, my chest filling with affection at the sleepy smile she gives me.

She fully wakes up on the drive home and I keep her hand clasped in mine the entire way. I'm aching for her as I pull into the driveway and open the garage. Was it just Monday that I stripped her down and carried her to my bed? It feels like forever as much as it does the blink of an eye.

She giggles as I lift her into my arms as soon as we're in the house. Her lips seal to mine, bringing my cock surging to life. I might just drop her on my couch and take her here first.

"What the fuck is going on here?" Jack's voice booms across the open living space, freezing both of us instantly.

Bri drops her legs, her brown eyes huge and already filled with tears.

"You have two seconds to let go of my daughter before I come over there and kick your ass."

Bri pushes my hands from her waist and turns to Jack. "Dad, what are you doing here?"

"I came straight here from the airport last night. I wanted to come home early and make sure you were okay. I guess I have my answer." His voice is venomous as he stalks toward me. "Have you been grooming her all her life for this moment?"

"What? No, Dad." She steps closer to him and further

from me. "Don't be ridiculous. We're both consenting adults here."

"I called you because I thought she'd be safe with you," he yells. "She just ended an engagement for Christ's sake."

"She is and always will be safe with me." I meet his eyes dead on. He can be mad, he has every right, but he won't pervert what's happening between Brianna and me.

"I should break your fucking hands for touching my daughter." He moves toward me quickly.

Brianna jumps in front of him to stop his progress, but he darts left. In doing so he accidentally knocks her over. She falls and cracks her forehead on the coffee table, a sickening crunch filling the air and then nothing.

We both run and drop down beside her. I roll her onto her back to make sure she's breathing and responsive as blood pours from a cut in her head. Pushing her hair away from her face, I cup the side of her head, already feeling a knot forming.

Jack tries to pry my hands from her, but I stop him with a searing look. "So fucking help me, Jack, if you interfere while I take care of her, I will call the police and file a goddamn report for assault."

He backs off, but I can feel his guilt and anger swirling around us. "Is she okay? Should we take her to a hospital?"

I tilt her head back and smack her cheek lightly. Her eyes flutter open and then wince closed.

"Sweetpea, I'm so sorry," Jack grabs her hand as a tear rolls down his cheek. "I didn't mean to knock you over."

"I know, Dad. It's okay." The blood is still running out of

her forehead so I stand to get a cloth and some ice while he watches over her.

"I think we need to take you to the hospital." Jack leans over and looks down at her gash. "Thomas, why isn't the bleeding stopping?"

"Because it's a head wound." I kneel down on her other side, but he's hovering over her. "Move aside so I can see what I need to do."

The gash is about an inch long, but fairly narrow. I doubt it needs stitches, a butterfly bandage should do the job. "I'm going to go grab my first aid kit," I say to Bri. "Hold this ice on your forehead to help the swelling and stop the bleeding."

"Dad, help me up."

I listen as Bri and her father talk quietly and when I come back into the room she's sitting on the edge of one of my kitchen chairs with him clutching her hand and apologizing profusely.

"I'll clean the cut and use a butterfly bandage to hold the wound together. It doesn't look like it'll need any stitches."

"Are you sure? It keeps bleeding." Jack interjects.

"Yes, I'm fucking sure, Jack. I am a goddamn doctor. Shut your mouth or go somewhere else."

"Thomas, easy," Bri whispers. "He feels awful."

"He should feel awful. It was fucking reckless. You could have been hurt worse."

"I'm fine. What's making me upset is watching and listening to you two fight."

"I'd say I'm sorry, but I'm not a liar. I'm fucking pissed." I finish cleaning the area with antiseptic wipes. "Can you hold your hair back?"

"Yes." She pulls her hair back and I look at her pupils, both of which look normal. Hopefully there's no concussion. I place the bandage over the wound with a clenched jaw.

"Okay, Bri." Jack grabs her hand and pulls her to her feet. "Let's go home."

"You're not taking her anywhere." I step between them. "Over my dead body does she leave this house tonight. She needs to be watched."

"Don't tempt me." Jack is about two inches shorter than me, but slightly bulkier. If this comes to blows we're evenly matched. "If she needs to be monitored, I'll take her to the hospital. Otherwise, I'm perfectly capable as her father to take care of her at home."

"That bump on her head says otherwise," I shoot back.

We go back and forth arguing as Bri sits down. I shoot her concerned looks every few minutes and I see Jack doing the same thing. After a few minutes, she stands and tells us she's going to the bathroom. The arguing continues between us until I realize that she's been in the bathroom a little too long. I leave Jack still huffing and grumbling and walk to the half bath off the kitchen that I saw her go toward.

When I get there, the door is wide open and the light is off, but the front door is cracked a bit. I run out to the front yard and see the pedestrian gate is open.

Fuck!

"Jack!" I yell. "She left."

"What?" He comes running. "Where would she go?"

14

BRIANNA

Is it the smartest thing to jump on the first flight from LA to DC with a likely concussion and nothing packed aside from what's in your purse? No, probably not. But I did it anyway and now I'm laying in bed next to my best friend eating ice cream and talking about how stupid men are.

Sara has her hair pulled up in a bonnet while she demolishes a pint of vanilla bean ice cream and keeps shooting sideways glances at me. She dropped everything as soon as I called her from LAX, and when she picked me up at the airport, she was ready with every type of comfort food, a list of movies we haven't gotten around to watching and bottles of my favorite wines.

"What are you going to do?" she asks between bites.

"I'm going to get drunk, pass out, and then go to brunch with you tomorrow and get drunk again."

I honestly didn't come here to do anything but forget about the past week. I want to bask in the solitude that is Sara's apartment, go to some museums, and hit up some bars. It's a pretty simple plan.

I definitely don't want to think about strong arms and long fingers. Or hauntingly beautiful green eyes and dark hair with hints of silver at the temples. I don't want to think about how for the first time in my life I felt like someone got me.

"That works for me but what are you going to do about Thomas? And your dad?"

"Nothing." I grab the cabernet beside me and take a drink, straight from the bottle. "Our little tryst ended as soon as we walked in the door and Dad saw us."

"Are you sure?"

"Sara," I whine. "I didn't come here to talk about it."

"You've been talking about it nonstop." She points at me with her spoon. "You're just pissy because I'm asking questions that you aren't ready to confront."

I scowl at her and pull my hood up. "I just don't know."

"Well, I actually think you do know. Let's work through it. Do you miss Trevor?"

My brows slam together as I look at her. I haven't even thought of him in days. "Not a bit. And I'm slightly pissed that you never called me on that sham of a relationship before."

"I didn't want to overstep." She holds her hands up. "But I am going to call you on your bullshit now."

"Of course you are."

"You look different after only a week with Thomas. You feel different. Your whole vibe is brighter and happier."

"It's just good dick."

"So go get some more of that good dick." She stands from the bed. "Get it anywhere he'll give it to you, which from what you've told me so far is any-fucking-where. You don't take a knee in the first quarter."

"He and Dad were fighting." I point to my forehead. "Almost about to go to physical blows. I don't want that for them. Especially after Thomas opened up about being a widower and bonding with Dad over that."

"Babe." She sits down beside me., "Don't you think the damage has been done?"

I bite down on my lip and look out her window. I can just about see the top of the Washington Monument from here. It's lit up stark white against the midnight sky.

"Bri," she says, pulling my attention away from the window. "Take your dad and recent relationship out of the picture. If Thomas had just walked into the bar as a stranger and picked you up, would you still be with him?"

"Yes." There is not a doubt in my mind.

"Think about how close you've gotten over the past week. How you've opened up to him in ways you've never opened up to anyone. Can you really walk away? Your dad will always love you regardless and if Thomas is as amazing as you say he is, he'll win Jack back over."

Her phone buzzes on the dresser for the fifth time in an hour.

"Do you need to get that?"

"No." She scowls at the phone. "They can wait."

She's been a little too into my drama this weekend. It's almost as if she's deflecting. I look back and forth between her and the phone again. She reads the look in my eyes and shakes her head at my unspoken questions. I let it go, for now.

"I know. Everything you're saying makes sense, but what if it doesn't work. What if I go back and things are just an even bigger mess. What if he doesn't even want me?"

"Turn your phone back on." She grabs my phone from my purse and tosses it to me. "I bet you brunch tomorrow that he's been blowing you up."

"I bet there will be more messages from my dad than Thomas."

"You're on." She nods at me. "Check it."

I turn the phone on and set it between us on the bed. A few seconds after, it loads to the home screen, text after text and dozens of missed calls show. I open my dad's text chain first.

DAD: Where are you?

Dad: Did you go home?

Dad: We just got here and you aren't here. Where are you??

Dad: Brianna Lucia

Dad: We are worried

Dad: Come home now

Dad: I'll put a hold on your credit card

Dad: I love you and hope you know bumping into you was an accident

Dad: Bri

Dad: I'm calling Sara

Dad: Thomas and I will stop fighting

"ELEVEN TEXTS FROM YOUR DAD." She picks up my phone and opens missed calls. "Fifteen missed calls."

I grab the phone back and note sixteen missed calls from Thomas. Looks like I'm losing the bet.

THOMAS: Bri, come home

Thomas: Where did you go, Siren?

Thomas: We're going to your dad's house

Thomas: I hope you are there and okay

Thomas: You aren't here <heartbreak emoji>

Thomas: As your doctor I insist you check in

Thomas: Siren

Thomas: Your dad and I have worked things out

Thomas: Come home

Thomas: To my home

Thomas: It's empty and cold without you

Thomas: I think I'm falling in love with you

Thomas: Please come home

Thomas: By the way, Jack agrees about the Venice Beach house

Thomas: If you don't text or call me back within the next day I'm transferring the deed in your name

. . .

"HE's IN LOVE WITH YOU." She looks up at me with hearts in her eyes.

"It's lust."

"He's almost fifty years old; he knows what love feels like."

"Whatever." She rolls her eyes and grabs her own phone which is buzzing again. She slams her thumb down on decline and shuts her phone off. "The rest of the time you're here, no phones for either of us. At least until I go back to work on Monday."

"Deal."

IT's Tuesday evening and I'm seeing Sara for the first time since she left for work Monday morning when I hear a knock at the door. She's in the shower so I pop my head in to let her know.

"Hey, someone's at the door. Are you expecting a delivery?"

"No, but answer it, just in case it's a messenger or something."

I bend down and scoop Jack, her cat, into my arms so he doesn't dart out of the door. She told me her peep hole has been fogged over since she moved in so I don't bother checking before I pull the door open.

The last thing I expect to see is Thomas standing there. He's a disheveled mess, a salt and pepper beard has started growing in, and for once, he looks his age. I stare at him, startled and confused by how he found me. Dad doesn't even have Sara's address.

He pushes the door all the way open and walks past me into the apartment. With one hand he closes the door and with the other he pushes me against the wall. I set Jack down right as Thomas slams his body and mouth against mine.

He groans as I open for him, his tongue plunging angrily past my lips and dueling with my own. His fingers dig into my hips in a punishing grip that will leave bruises. I slide my fingers into his hair and tug. The violence in our embrace pulls every bit of savagery out of me and pouring it into our kiss.

Fuck, I missed him.

His hand snakes under my shirt and palms my bare breast. He pinches and twists my nipple painfully, swallowing the noise that comes from my throat at the sensation. It's part moan, part whimper, and all desire.

"Where are you sleeping?" he asks against my mouth.

"Sharing the bed with Sara."

He groans in disappointment as we keep kissing.

"Bestie, this isn't how you tip a messenger," Sara jokes as she runs from the bathroom into her bedroom.

The door closes quietly behind her and it's enough to break the spell between us. His green eyes search mine like he's trying to solve life's greatest mystery.

He rests his forehead against mine and takes a deep breath. "I'll get us a hotel room. We can talk there. Grab your things."

I knock on Sara's door to make sure she's dressed before I walk in. I enter and close it behind me when she tells me to come in. Her eyes are huge and excited.

"He is hot," she whisper-exclaims.

"I know," I whisper-yell back at her. "How did he find me?"

"You'll have to ask him."

"He's taking me to a hotel."

"Good. Go." She shoos me out as she hands me my purse. Then she grabs me back and pulls me in for a tight hug. "I'm definitely going to need details."

Thomas is staring a hole into the bedroom door when I open it.

"I'm ready." I stand there awkwardly as his gaze lingers on my forehead. "I haven't touched the bandage, I wasn't sure what to do."

"If you would have returned one of my calls or texts, I could have given you instructions." He pulls me into his arms and holds me, sniffing my hair. "Where's your bag?"

"I don't have one. I left your house and went straight to LAX. I bought a few pairs of new underwear, but I've been borrowing Sara's clothes the whole time I've been here."

"You flew commercial with a fresh head injury?" he growls, clearly upset with my decision making.

I'm about to launch into my reasoning for why I left the way I did, but now that he's here, in front of me, looking sexy as sin I need him alone. Now.

"Let's go somewhere we can talk privately."

"Yeah, I've got work to do," Sara calls from her bedroom. "I don't want to listen to this."

I grab his hand, leading him out the apartment and down the narrow set of stairs to the lobby. Her building has an elevator, but it's old and scares me. I'm about to order an Uber when Thomas pulls me to the corner and into the backseat of a black town car. Because, of course, he has a driver on standby.

He tells the driver to take us to the Intercontinental and then reaches for me. With one tug on my thigh he has us pressed together tightly in the backseat.

"You sure do like to run, you know that?" he whispers into my ear. "I've spent the past four days alternating between worried sick and plotting all the ways I'm going to make sure you never run away again."

He cups my cheek and turns me to face him. "I might just chain you to my bed for all eternity. Turn you into a truly kept woman. A sex slave. My slave." He bites my earlobe. "Mine."

My insides turn from mush to boiling hot with the sharp pain of his teeth. All my feminism just flew out the window with his possessive words.

"When we get checked in, the first thing I'm going to do is fuck you like my life depends on it because at this point, I really think it might. I took another week off to hunt you down. I haven't taken more than a day off work at one time in ten years. You're driving me crazy, Siren." He gives a wolfish smile as we drive past the White House. "I guess you really are one, with the way I've become obsessed with you."

It takes less than five minutes from the time the driver drops us in front of the hotel until I'm pressed against the wall of the elevator. I can feel Thomas' hard length against my stomach as he dominates my mouth with his own. He kisses me like he'll never get enough, like I'm his oxygen. When the doors slide open he yanks me along behind him roughly.

Every part of me is burning for him.

As soon as the hotel room door closes behind us, his mouth is fused to mine again. He pulls my shirt over my head and pushes my shorts down my legs. I work his shirt off while we stumble through the dark to the bed. It's a frantic race to fuck all the emotions we've experienced the past few days out of our system.

My legs hit the side of the bed and I fall backwards while he climbs on top, pulling me up to the pillows. His lips leave mine to kiss and lick and bite a trail down my body to the apex of my thighs. His hands hook around my panties as he pulls them off and tosses them aside.

Then his tongue laps at me, sliding up and down my slit with deviant intent. My body arches against his mouth as he bites my clit, giving me the perfect amount of pain with my pleasure. I beg for his fingers, the way he finds that spot deep inside and sends my orgasms straight through the air.

"No." He sits up between my thighs. "Your g-spot is a reward you haven't earned."

He slowly pulls his belt through the loops and lays it out beside us before stripping his pants and boxer briefs off. Ever so slowly, he crawls up my body until he's kneeling over my chest.

"Wrists," he commands as he grabs his belt.

I hold them up and together for him as he wraps it around and cinches them together.

"This is *my* body to play with tonight." He pushes my hands over my head. "Leave them until I say otherwise."

"Yes, Dr." I intended to use a teasing tone, but instead the taunt came out as a sexy whisper.

"Oh, Siren. You don't know what you're in for." He strokes himself as he looks down darkly at me. "Open those pouty lips for my cock."

I immediately open for him as he guides his dick down my throat. He grips the headboard with one hand and my hair with the other. At first, his pace is slow and steady. When I hollow my cheeks around him, he groans my name. His control snaps when I moan and do it again. He thrusts into my mouth with bruising intensity.

I can feel his release building as his cock jerks in my mouth. Right before he comes he pulls out from between my lips and slides back down my body. Before I can formulate my complaint at his hasty retreat he's flipping me onto my stomach and lifting my hips in the air.

My arms are still stretched and bound above my head, my chest pressed onto the mattress, the scratchy hotel bed linens abrasive against my hardened nipples. The combination of my discomfort heightens the pleasure as he slowly works his way into me.

With a painfully unhurried pace, he glides back and forth inside me. Once he fully seats himself, he circles his pelvis against my cunt, somehow finding the place inside me that he knows how to work effortlessly.

He repeats the motion over and over until I'm trembling under him only to pull all the way out, leaving me aching and needy. His fingers find my clit, teasing me right back to the precipice before withdrawing.

I whimper and lift my hips even higher, begging silently for the release I know he can give me. Then I feel his tongue on me again. He circles my pussy relentlessly, then lazily makes his way down to my clit, but only teases back and forth, taunting me with desire and need.

"Thomas." His name is a plea.

"Yes?" I feel his breath against my heated skin.

"Please?" I beg.

"Please, what?" he asks, his voice sounding so innocent.

"Please let me come. I need it. I need you."

"Are you ever going to run from me again?" He licks me.

"No," I whimper. "I'll never run again."

"You'll use the Venice house next year." Another lick.

"Yes." I'd honestly agree to murder at this point. "Anything you want. Please, just fuck me like you own me."

A growl tears from his chest. "I do own you."

He slams into me hard enough to rock the bed against the wall. His fingers dig into my hips as he holds them up at an unnatural but incredible angle. Just as before, his cock hits that place deep inside me and sends me careening through a kaleidoscope of pleasure. I come so hard I see multicolor stars behind my eyes.

Thomas keeps going. His panted breaths and the sound of his skin slapping against mine fills the room with our sexual debauchery. I gasp as his hand comes down on my ass cheek, heat racing from the impact straight to my core. His other hand circles around and pinches my clit making a second, unexpected orgasm tear through me just as the first subsides. I feel him jerk inside me, his cum filling me and marking me as his.

"Fuck," he chants over and over.

He pulls out of me and collapses to my side. His deft fingers unbuckle the belt and free my arms, which are tingly and numb. Then he draws me over to him, laying me partially across his chest while we both come back down.

"Mine," he says as he gives me a tender kiss.

"Yours," I agree.

EPILOGUE

THOMAS

TWO YEARS LATER

"Thomas? Can you come in here?" Bri calls from our ensuite as I strip out of my scrubs in the closet.

"Sure." My bare feet pad across the marble as I cross to her.

She's looking down at the vanity and paying no attention to me as I come from behind and wrap my arms around her. She's just gotten home as well, still in her sexy pencil skirt and cashmere sweater. She recently started working as in-house counsel for an environmental non-profit working on water rights and preservation.

We were married in a small backyard ceremony ten months ago, the weekend after she graduated from law school with about a dozen guests present. Then we flew down to Brazil to celebrate with her avó, her maternal grandma, and the rest of that side of the family. Then we honeymooned in Argentina.

I kiss her cheek, trying to get her to look up, and that's when I see it. Or rather them.

Four pregnancy tests.

Six pink lines.

One digital read-out saying 'pregnant.'

Joy ricochets through me. I splay my hands out protectively over her belly. Her teary eyes meet mine in the mirror.

"I'm pregnant," she whispers as the first tear falls.

"You are," I agree.

We've been trying for a while with no luck, not incredibly surprising considering my age and her family history. Next month we were due to start fertility treatments.

She spins in my arms and locks hers around my neck as she sobs into my bare chest. My eyes burn as I cling to her. My happiness is bittersweet. I've been here before and can already feel my anxiety climb as I hold her.

I would not survive losing her and our baby.

"Are you okay?" She leans back and cups my face while her eyes search mine.

"Yes." I turn my head and kiss her palm. "I'm over the moon excited. Truthfully, I know I'm going to be an overprotective monster. You're just going to have to deal with it."

"I'm okay with that." She kisses me long and thoroughly. "I'm going to have our baby," she says when we break apart. "I'm growing a human inside me. It's so weird to think about."

I drop down to my knees and pull her skirt down her hips, exposing her soft belly. Her fingers make their familiar slide into my hair as I kiss below her belly button and whisper promises to our growing child.

"I'll retire to take care of the baby," I say as our eyes meet.

BRIANNA

ONE YEAR LATER

I THOUGHT Thomas was crazy when he said he'd retire to take care of our son. He had never been ready to even consider retirement before. For the longest time I didn't take him seriously. Then one day I came home from work and he laid a contract in front of me to review. The sale of his plastic surgery practice to another surgeon.

My jaw dropped. At how serious he was and how much he was selling the practice for. I could quit working and our lifestyle wouldn't change in the least, but I can't do that.

Simon, our son, is three months old and I've already gone back to work. There is a pipeline in the works that has the potential to harm an entire ecosystem so I was needed.

Watching Thomas walk back and forth across the patio with Simon in his arms as he quiets him down for the night never gets old. I don't like to miss meals with my guys, but sometimes it can't be avoided. I know Dad was over here earlier though, he begrudgingly accepted Thomas and my relationship and since having Simon he's around more than ever.

Walking quietly to avoid waking Simon if he's already sleeping, I join them on the patio. Thomas has him swaddled in a muslin blanket with tiny stethoscopes printed all over it. He's convinced he's raising the next top surgeon. In fact, I've caught him reading medical journals over baby books aloud on more than one occasion.

It's quirky and cute. Completely on brand for Thomas as a father. He's beyond amazing with Simon. The way he's managed to turn our tiny three month old into his little bestie is as heartwarming as it is sexy.

There were definitely challenging times while I was pregnant. From the moment we found out, he was on constant high alert. He went so far as to beg me to use a driver while I was pregnant. I gently pointed out that either way, I'd be in a car. We compromised with constant communication throughout the day while we were each at our respective jobs.

"Hand him over and I'll put him down." I hold my hands out and smile down at my sweet baby boy as Thomas gently passes him to me. Simon's dark green eyes open slowly and he gives me a sleepy smile.

"I'll clean up while you nurse him." Thomas gives me a kiss and slips inside the house.

I follow him inside and walk into the nursery, sitting down and lifting my shirt, getting us both situated while I rock in the glider. The soft glow of the nightlight is the only illumination in the quiet, dark space.

After a few minutes of watching him nurse, I look up to see Thomas leaning against the door jam, watching us. I can't see his face, but I can feel his overwhelming love. He loves us in the most profoundly all-consuming way.

"I think we should make another," he says as I slip past him into the hall after laying Simon down. "Tonight."

I blink in surprise. We haven't talked about having another, although I'm definitely down for more babies. "Really?"

"Yeah, really." He grabs the base of my ponytail and angles my head back for access. "I want to plant another baby in you right now."

"Then take me to bed, Dr. Brennan."

ACKNOWLEDGMENTS

I will always and forever thank my family for supporting me in this dream of writing books. Without your understanding I would not be able to do this. Without your willingness to step in while I need to lose myself in a story there would be no books, no outlet for me to tell these stories. To my four incredible children, your love and pride in what I do means more than I will ever be able to adequately describe.

This one is really for the incredible friends I've made on social media, particularly Booktok. There are honestly too many of you to shout out individually. You guys and your creativity blow me away daily. I'm so glad I've become friends with so many of you.

Miranda. You amazing, incredible friend. We didn't do as much together on this project, but you were always there, cheering me on and kicking my ass when I needed it. Your aggressive love and belief in me, my ability to tell a story, and my worth as human is so treasured. No one gives me tough love like you do.

Karley, you are such an incredible alpha reader. The way you gas me up and fall so hard so my characters and plots never fails to keep me moving through the muckiest part of imposter syndrome. I would not be here without you.

Hayley, you came into my life at the exact moment I

needed you most. From being an enthusiastic fan to now someone I speak to every day. I am so deeply grateful to have you as one of my closest (and yet so far away) friends. Talon is yours.

Chloe, the better half of NiChloe. I'm so glad to have grown this friendship with you. Watching you the past year has me feeling like a proud big sister. Thank you so much for everything you do for me.

Darby and Claire, you powerhouse duo. This book wouldn't be as strong as it is without you. Your insights are always spot on and I'm looking forward to working with you in the future. Not to mention your legendary GIF game. No one compares!

To my beta team, thank you all so much. Jen, your video give me life and I make my family watch them on the big television about 100 times. You are incredible. Sheri, Valerie, Rachel, you three have been there from the beginning and mean the world to me. Your insights and questions always help me see my manuscript from a different perspective and I thank you for it.

Kelsey, I adore you and can't wait to watch you take the fantasy world by storm!

Brianna, I hope you love living vicariously through this story. What a perfect time for you to hop on board as my PA. It's barely been a month but the assistance from you has already eased my workload and allowed me to focus on writing. So incredibly thankful for you!

To my street team, you all are incredible. Your help pushing my content on social media, encouragement, and love for the characters and world I create are immeasurably meaningful. I could not do this without you. You are each amazing and special people to me.

Finally, to my readers! Damn. Thank you so, so much for staying with me. I see you reading, I see you posting reviews and sharing content. I honestly cannot thank you enough for trusting me to take you on these journeys and introduce you to the chaos in my mind.

EVERYONE LOVES A SCANDAL

In a city obsessed with power, only those willing to go low
ever come out on top.

Book Two of the Forbidden Love Series
coming in late 2022

Turn the page to read an excerpt of your next
book boyfriend obsession.

SAVAGE LOVE

Chapter One
Elle

There comes a time in every girl's life where she just has to put her foot down along with a nine iron through the windshield of her twin sister's ex-boyfriend's Ferrari Spider. Ten minutes ago we all hanging out at an abandoned granite mine, celebrating our nineteenth birthday when everyone's cell phones lit up with notifications. Life was great until I opened the video and saw a video of my sister mid sexual act.

The first person I made eye contact with was our little brother, Michael, who was already striding off in search of the limp dick waste of life who was lucky to have spent one second with our sister. Nora and I are nearly identical except I have one green eye and one blue and her body is full and curvy compared to my thin and strong physique. She is sweet and smart and everything good that I am not.

When I look at her I see she's still watching, her face twisted in pain and horror. Luckily our cousins, Sloane and Alina, are already beside her. I walk over to her and pull the phone from her stiff fingers. Her eyes, a glacial blue like our mother's, are glassy with unshed tears that she blinks away.

"You have nothing to be ashamed of," I tell her as I lean my forehead against hers. "Jace is going to pay for this."

I'll be meting out justice Volkov style, cold, fast, and as savage as possible. While Nora got all the good, I got all the crazy. All the Russian ferocity from my dad's side of the family mixed with my mom's stubborn refusal to ever bow to anyone. I look at Sloane who has a comforting arm around Nora and turn on my heel in search of the fucker who's life I'm about to destroy.

When I find him he is on the ground under Michael's bloodied fist. I don't step in until Jace is on the verge of losing consciousness, not because I give a fuck about his health but because I want him to watch what I plan to do. We don't know if he's the person who sent the video but from the angle I know he was the one who filmed it. I also know Nora would never have agreed to it.

A crowd has circled the scene and no one is stepping in. Most of them are probably afraid, not just of Michael or me but our family as whole. I fish Jace's keys out of his pockets and toss them to Brady, our cousin.

"Bring his car over here," I say as he catches them. Then I look down at his glazed over eyes, he's bleeding pretty heavily from a cut in his forehead and it looks like he might be missing a tooth. "You are so stupid." I stand and put my foot on his chest.

"You good here?" Michael asks. "I want to go check on Nora real quick."

I nod at him and dig my stiletto into Jace's ribs. "I'm fine."

"Hold the show for me," he flashes me a smile identical to our father's, right down to the dimple, before jogging off to find Nora.

I look back down at the pathetic waste of life below me. "I'm going to enjoy this, Jace. I hope you know that. You were lucky to even breathe the same air as my sister. I always knew you would peak in high school, how fucking sad."

The crowd parts as Brady drives the car up to where I'm standing. He gets out and tosses me one of his golf clubs. I catch it in the air and jump onto the hood.

"Pick him so he can watch." I make sure tho drag my heels over the obnoxious red paint while I wait for him to look up at me. "Do you know what makes me angry?" I look at Jace and wait for a response.

He stubbornly refuses to say a word.

"Oh, big mistake." I laugh as I bring the club down on the windshield of the car with all the force I can. The sound of glass breaking and shouts from the crowd fill the air. "Ready to answer the question yet?"

"You're a fucking psycho." This idiot can barely stand and he's still being a punk.

"Yes," I look at him patronizingly, "this isn't news. I warned you what would happen if you hurt my sister." I bring the club down again, shattering more of the windshield.

"That's my dad's car," Jace is finally starting to look worried. "I get it. Point made."

"You don't sound sincere, Jace." I look around trying to find some other way to punish him. My eyes land on a pile of bricks. I jump off the hood and walk over to the pile lifting a few of them into my arms.

"No, Elle." Jace shakes his head, wincing at the pain I'm sure it causes. "Stop. You don't understand. Don't."

"Too late." I slide behind the wheel of the car, slightly upset at the thought of ruining such a good car but consequences must be faced. I turn the car on and slip it into neutral. It's about twenty feet to the cliff and straight down into one hundred and fifty feet of water.

Brady and Sloane both look a little uneasy. Nora and Alina are no where to be seen so I assume they went home. I make and hold eye contact with Michael who nods at me in complete solidarity. He comes and stands behind the trunk, waiting for me to put the bricks over the gas pedal.

"Elle! Stop! It's not funny anymore. I'm sorry, okay? I was so mad about the break up that I wasn't thinking clearly." One of his eyes is already swollen shut. "I just loved her so much, you know? When she broke up with me I lost my shit. I wasn't thinking clearly. I-"

"I don't care about your excuses." I walk back to join Michael as Brady flanks my other side. It doesn't take much to push it over the edge. Murmurs and muffled laughter are the only sound until the car splashes down into the pit of black water.

Jace drops back down to his knees and runs his fingers through his hair as the taillights disappear into the dark depths. He mumbles something incoherent as his head shakes back and forth slowly. Then he lifts his gaze to mine, his eyes resigned and empty. "You have no idea what you just did."

I walk past him without saying anything. The adrenaline high of protecting my family is fading quickly. I just want to get home and check on Nora. I cut through the crowd with my head held high, I'm not ashamed of who I am.

\#

"Elle!" My father's voice booms from the other side of my bedroom door along with his strong fist against the wood. "Family brunch in ten minutes."

I crack one eye open and fumble for my phone. The lock screen is full of notifications I don't want to deal with so I set it back down and fling the covers off. Normally I'd go super casual with my clothing choice on a Sunday morning but today is our actual birthday. The entire family is here, my aunts and uncles, cousins, and grandparents. For that reason I grab a pair of jeans and a green tank top.

I showered when I came home from the party last night so I take my hair out of the two braids I put it in and finger comb the waves out. My morning routine only takes five minutes. I'm dressed and walking down the hall when Nora's door opens.

I wait for her at the top of the stairs. She's wearing black shorts and an oversize off the shoulder shirt. Her hair is hanging loose around her shoulders, falling nearly all the way down her back. I know what she's doing, hiding behind her hair. Her figure is fuller than mine, soft where I'm all hard muscle and lean lines. She thinks the only beautiful thing about herself is her glossy black hair but she's so much more than that.

I wish we could switch places for a day so she could see herself through my eyes. How gorgeous her bright blue eyes are in the bright sunlight. How just her very presence can calm my chaos.

"Stop." Her voice is quiet but stern. She knows exactly what I was just thinking and it annoys her.

"Morning, wombie," I say with a bright smile, using the nickname we gave each other years ago. "How'd you sleep?"

"What is this 'sleep' you speak of?" A yawn slips from her lips as she says it.

"Sleep is what happens when you close your eyes and let your mind drift away on a sea of violent fantasies." I sweep my hand out dramatically.

An amused snort comes from behind us. "You would, psycho."

I turn and look at my little brother, annoyed because I have to tilt my head back now. He's already taller than our dad and he's barely seventeen. "Put some clothes on, pleb."

He smirks and pulls a shirt on. He's barefoot and in a pair of athletic shorts. His hair hasn't even been combed. I doubt he's even brushed his teeth. "Happy birthday," he leans down and gives Nora a hug, "to my favorite sister."

I give him the finger over my shoulder and start walking again. "She was mine first." I'm swept up, spun, and tossed over his shoulder like I'm light as a feather.

"Happy birthd—" His breath whooshes out as my fist

collides with his kidney. "Day. Fuck. Good one." He sets me down so he can rub his back.

"You guys are animals," Nora rolls her eyes but can't fight the grin that appears. "Didn't you work that aggression out last night?"

"Nope."

"Fuck no," I answer with a hand to my chest. "You know my aggression replenishes overnight. It's like you don't know me at all."

The three of us walk into the kitchen together. Our dad is talking to our uncles in the corner of the room over cups of coffee. They have their heads together looking down at a phone. Uncle Griff looks up first and smiles at us.

"Here come the birthday girls." He holds his tattooed arm out and Nora tucks into his side for a hug.

"Come here, trouble," Uncle Levi says to me as he wraps me in a hug.

"Where's everyone else?" I ask when he releases me.

"Out on the patio."

"Nora," Dad says after giving us both hugs. "Go on out. I want to talk to these two," he points at Michael and me.

She looks at me with a brief flash of uncertainty. I give her a slight nod so she'll know I'm good. I have Michael to back me up anyway. I don't regret one thing I did last night and I'd do it all over again. When I look over at my brother he has a hard expression on his face. He clearly shares my sentiment about our actions.

"Tell us everything that happened last night," Dad commands.

"Someone shared a video of an intimate moment

between Nora and Jace." I watch my Dad's face tighten, lines bracket his mouth and eyes as his infamous glare emerges. "It was clear from the activity and angle that Jace took the video."

"That little fucker," Levi growls.

"Is broken and bloody today," Michael says quickly.

They all nod in approval.

"And down a car." I tilt my head and look my dad in the eye. "I pushed his Ferrari into the mine at the Abyss."

Dad tries to hide the fact that he's secretly proud of both of us by scrubbing his hand over his face. Levi gives us both a smirk but Griff looks troubled. Dad notices and they share a loaded look.

"What?" I ask as my eyes bounce back and forth between them.

"The Ferrari wasn't Jace's car, it belongs to his father."

This news doesn't phase me. "Just take it out of my trust." I shrug, completely unbothered at the thought of losing that money. I'd still do it all over again.

"No." Dad shakes his head. "We're not paying them off."

"Jace broke several laws filming and sharing a s—" For second the time in twenty minutes my fist connects with Michael's body. Our dad and uncles do not need to hear the words 'sex tape' in conjunction with arguably the best, most responsible one of all of us. "All I'm saying is, he's actually getting off easy. A lost car versus a son on the sex offender list for the rest of his life."

"Go on out," Dad nudges us both toward the door, "we need to talk through some stuff."

Michael and I both hesitate but it's clear by the stern

looks on all their faces that we're not going to be clued in to what they are talking about. We walk out the back door to the chaos of our family all together. The younger cousins are all out playing soccer or in the treehouse. Nora, Alina, and Sloane are sitting at a table beside our mom and aunts. Michael splits off from me to go hang with Brady.

"Morning honey," Mom says as she stands to give me a hug. "Happy birthday."

"Thanks mom." I squeeze her tightly, burying my face in her blonde hair. I used to be so sad that I didn't inherit the golden strands and instead take mostly after Dad's side of the family.

She sits back down, making room for me on the bench. We all talk about plans for the rest of the summer. Alina is going to spend all her time in city with Griff and Claire, interning at their media company. Sloane always volunteers at the summer camp Levi runs in the Catskills. Nora and I will be spending most of the summer at our grandmother's estate in Ireland with our grandparents. Today is our last day all together until we go to college in the fall.

Continue reading:

Savage Love

ABOUT THE AUTHOR

Nichole is a dreamer who on a random day in May 2019 decided she was going to write a book. Those dreams became words which became a book which have turned into multiple books. When she's not writing, she's probably reading or playing snack bitch to her four children. She's a plant obsessed, tea sipping, wine drinking millennial with a deep love for romance, politics, and science fiction.

ALSO BY NICHOLE GREENE

Made in the USA
Middletown, DE
17 October 2023

40977395R00090